SNOWBLIND JUSTICE

—

CINDI MYERS

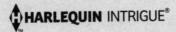

For Gay and Reed.

ISBN-13: 978-1-335-60471-2

Snowblind Justice

Copyright © 2019 by Cynthia Myers

Recycling programs for this product may not exist in your area.

Printed in U.S.A.

www.Harlequin.com

Cindi Myers is the author of more than fifty novels. When she's not crafting new romance plots, she enjoys skiing, gardening, cooking, crafting and daydreaming. A lover of small-town life, she lives with her husband and two spoiled dogs in the Colorado mountains.

Books by Cindi Myers

Harlequin Intrigue

Eagle Mountain Murder Mystery: Winter Storm Wedding

Ice Cold Killer
Snowbound Suspicion
Cold Conspiracy
Snowblind Justice

Eagle Mountain Murder Mystery

Saved by the Sheriff
Avalanche of Trouble
Deputy Defender
Danger on Dakota Ridge

The Ranger Brigade: Family Secrets

Murder in Black Canyon
Undercover Husband
Manhunt on Mystic Mesa
Soldier's Promise
Missing in Blue Mesa
Stranded with the Suspect

The Men of Search Team Seven

Colorado Crime Scene
Lawman on the Hunt
Christmas Kidnapping
PhD Protector

Visit the Author Profile page at Harlequin.com.

CAST OF CHARACTERS

Emily Walker—Travis Walker's younger sister has put her graduate studies on hold to help with the wedding, but her previous acquaintance with the main suspect in a series of murders has involved her in the case more than she would like.

Brodie Langtry—The investigator with the Colorado Bureau of Investigation once proposed to Emily Walker, only to have her turn him down. When his hunt for the killer brings him into her life again, he's determined to make up for past mistakes.

Travis Walker—The groom-to-be and county sheriff takes the murders perpetrated on his watch personally.

Lacy Milligan—The bride-to-be is determined not to let snowstorms and a serial killer put a damper on her wedding.

The Ice Cold Killer—The serial killer is targeting women in and around Eagle Mountain and has everyone on edge. As his violence escalates, he comes closer and closer to Emily and the Walker family.

Chapter One

Snow sifted down over the town like a downy blanket, turning trash piles into pristine drifts, transforming mine ruins into nostalgic works of art, hiding ugliness and danger beneath a dusting of wedding-cake white.

The murderer lurked behind a veil of snow, fresh flakes hiding his tracks, muffling the sound of his approach, covering up the evidence of his crimes. Deep cold and furious blizzards kept others indoors, but the killer reveled in his mastery over the landscape. His pursuers thought he was soft, like them. They couldn't find him because they assumed conditions were too harsh for him to survive in the wilderness.

And all the while he was waiting, striking when the right opportunity presented itself, his intellect as much of a weapon as his muscles. The woman who lay before him now was a prime example. She hadn't hesitated to stop when he had flagged her down on the highway. He was merely a stranded motorist who needed help. He was good-looking and charming—what woman wouldn't want to help him?

By the time she realized his purpose, it was too late. Like the officials who tracked him, she had underestimated him. The lawmen doubted his ability to instill trust in his victims, and were awed by his talent for killing quickly and efficiently while leaving no trace.

He lifted the woman's inert body into the car, arranging it into an artful tableau across the seat. There was very little blood—none in the vehicle—and no fingerprints or other evidence for the sheriff and his deputies to trace. They would search and examine and photograph and question—and they would find nothing.

He shut the door to the car and trudged away as the snow began to fall harder, a sifting of sugar over the bloodstains on the side of the road, and over his footprints, and over the signs of a struggle in the older snow beside the highway. The killer ducked behind a wall of ice, and disappeared out of sight of the empty road. Wind blew the snow sideways, the flakes sticking to the knit mask he had pulled up over his face, but he scarcely felt the cold, too absorbed in the details of his latest killing, reveling in his skill at pulling it off—again.

There were no witnesses to his crime, and none to his getaway. The lawmen thought they were closing in on him because they had linked his name to his crimes. But they didn't realize he was the one drawing nearer and nearer to his goal. Soon he would claim his final victim—the woman who had brought him to Eagle Mountain in the first place. After he had taken her, he would disappear, leaving his pursuers to wonder at his daring. They would hate him more than ever, but some part of them would have to admire his genius.

"I FEEL LIKE I should apologize for seventeen-year-old Emily's poor taste in prom dresses." Emily Walker looked down at the dress she had unearthed from the back of her closet that morning—too short in the front, too long in the back, entirely too many ruffles and a very bright shade of pink.

"It will be fine as soon as we straighten out the hem and maybe take off a few ruffles." Lacy Milligan looked up from her position kneeling on the floor beside the chair Emily stood on, and tucked a lock of her sleek brown hair behind one ear. "You'll look great."

"Everyone is supposed to be looking at you when you walk down the aisle in that gorgeous bridal gown—not at the clashing train wreck of attendants at the front of the room," Emily said. Watching Lacy wouldn't be a hardship—she was gorgeous, and so was her dress. The same couldn't be said for the bridesmaids' makeshift ensembles. "Let's hope the highway reopens and the dresses you chose for your wedding can be delivered."

"Not just the dresses," Lacy said. "The wedding

favors and some of the decorations are waiting to be delivered, as well. Not to mention some of the guests." She returned to pinning the dress. "With less than a week to go, I can't risk waiting much longer to figure out how to use what we have here—including this dress." She inserted a pin in the hem of the skirt and sat back on her heels to study the results. "As it is, I may be going through the wedding shy one bridesmaid if the highway doesn't open soon."

"The road is going to open soon," Emily said. "The weather reports look favorable." Since the New Year, the southwest corner of Colorado had been hammered by a wave of snowstorms that had dumped more than six feet of snow in the mountains. The snow, and the avalanches that inevitably followed, had blocked the only road leading in and out of the small town of Eagle Mountain for most of the past month.

"Travis tried to talk me into delaying the wedding." Lacy sighed. "Not just because of the weather, but because of this serial killer business."

A serial murderer who had been dubbed the Ice Cold Killer had murdered six women in the area in the past few weeks. Lacy's fiancé—Emily's brother Sheriff Travis Walker—had been working practically 'round the clock to try to stop the elusive serial killer. Emily thought postponing the wedding until the killer was caught and the weather improved wasn't such a bad idea, but she wasn't a bride who had spent the past six months planning the ceremony and reception. "What did you tell him?" Emily asked.

"I told him I'm willing to postpone my honeymoon. I understand that being a sheriff's wife means putting my needs behind those of the town. And I've been patient—I really have. I haven't seen him in two days and I haven't complained at all. But Sunday is my wedding day. All I ask is that he be here for a few hours. The case will wait that long."

"It's not just Travis," Emily said. "Half the wedding party is law enforcement. There's Gage." Emily and Travis's brother was a sheriff's deputy. "Cody Rankin—he's technically on leave from the US Marshals office, but he's still working on the case. And Nate Harris—he's supposed to be off work from his job with the Department of Wildlife to recover from his ankle injury, but he's as busy as ever, from what I can tell. Oh, and Ryder Stewart—he's had plenty of time to help Travis, since most of his highway patrol territory is closed due to snow."

"Then they can be here for a few hours, too," Lacy said. "That may sound terribly selfish of me, but I put so much of my life on hold for the three years I was in prison. I don't want to wait any longer." Lacy had been wrongfully convicted of murdering her boss. She and Travis had fallen in love after he had worked to clear her name.

"Then you deserve the wedding you want, when you want it," Emily said. "I hope my brother was understanding."

"He was, after I whined and moaned a little bit." Lacy stood and walked around the chair to take in the dress from all sides. "I didn't tell him this, but another reason I want to go ahead with the wedding is that I'm beginning to be afraid the killer won't be caught. Travis and every other lawman in the area has been hunting this guy for weeks. It's like he's a ghost. Travis and Gage and the rest of them work so hard and the murderer just thumbs his nose at them."

"It's crazy." Emily climbed down off the chair and began helping Lacy gather up the sewing supplies. "At first I was terrified. Well, I guess I'm still terrified, but honestly, I'm also angry." She patted Lacy's shoulder. "Anyway, I'm not going to let the killer or the weather get me down. The weather is going to hold, the road will open and you'll have a beautiful wedding, without my fashion faux pas spoiling the day."

"I hope you're right and everyone I invited can be here," Lacy said.

"Who in the wedding party is still missing?" Emily asked.

"Paige Riddell. She recently moved to Denver with her boyfriend, Rob Allerton."

"Of course." Paige had run a bed-and-breakfast in town prior to moving away. "I never knew her well, but she seemed really nice."

"She is nice. And I really want her here for my wedding. But you can't fight nature, I guess, so we're going to make do no matter what." She turned to

Emily. "Thank you so much for everything you've done to help," she said. "Not just with the wedding preparations, but all the work you've put into entertaining the wedding guests who are already here. I forget that the weather has forced you to put your own life on hold, too."

Like everyone else who had been in town when the first blizzard struck, Emily had been stuck in Eagle Mountain for most of the past month. "The first few weeks I was on my winter break," she said. She was working on her master's at Colorado State University and was employed by the university as a teaching assistant and researcher. "It's just the last ten days that I've missed. Fortunately, the university has been very understanding, letting me complete some of my coursework and research online, delaying some other work and arranging for another researcher to teach my undergrad class until I get back."

"I'm glad," Lacy said. "Can you imagine having to delay your master's degree because of snow?"

"Snow has its upsides, too," Emily said. "That sleigh ride last week was a blast, and I'm looking forward to the bonfire Wednesday."

"Every party you've thrown has been a big success," Lacy said. "I'm sure most brides don't entertain their guests so lavishly."

"Well, everything has gone well except the scavenger hunt," Emily said. "I wouldn't call that a success."

"It's not your fault Fiona was murdered during

the party." Lacy hugged herself and shuddered. "I thought for sure Travis would catch the killer after that—he was so close, right here on the ranch."

Just like that, the conversation turned back to the Ice Cold Killer as the two friends remembered each of his victims—some of them locals they had known, a few tourists or newcomers they had never had a chance to meet. But every person who had fallen victim to the killer had been young and female, like Emily and Lacy. They didn't have to say it, but they were both keenly aware that they might have been one of the killer's victims—or they still might be.

Emily was relieved when the door to the sunroom, where they were working, opened and Bette Fuller, one of Lacy's best friends and the caterer for the wedding, breezed in. Blonde and curvy, Bette always lit up the room, and today she was all smiles. "Rainey just got back from town and she says the highway is open." Bette hugged Lacy. "I know this is what you've been waiting for."

"Is Rainey sure?" Lacy asked.

"Rainey isn't one for spreading rumors or telling lies," Emily said. The ranch cook was even more stone-faced and tight-lipped than Travis. Emily looked down at the dress she was wearing, now bristling with pins and marks made with tailor's chalk. "Maybe I won't have to wear this old thing after all."

"Rainey said there was a line of delivery trucks coming into town," Bette said. "Which is a good thing, since the stores are low on everything."

"I'm going to call Paige and tell her and Rob to drop everything and drive over right now—before another avalanche closes the road," Lacy said. "And I need to check with the florist and look at the tracking for the bridesmaids' dresses and the wedding favors and the guest book I ordered, too."

"I can help you with some of that," Bette said.

"You two go on," Emily said. "I'll finish cleaning up in here." The prom dress—pins and all—could go back in the closet. If she was lucky, she'd never have to put it on again.

As she gathered up the clutter from around the room, she thought of all the work that went into weddings. This was only her second time serving as a bridesmaid, and she was looking forward to the ceremony, though she was a little nervous, too. Mostly, she hoped she wouldn't get too emotional. Weddings were supposed to be hopeful occasions, but they always made her a little melancholy, wondering what her own wedding would have been like—and how different her life might have turned out if she had accepted the one proposal she had had.

Who was she kidding? If she had agreed to marry that man, it would have been a disaster. She had been far too young for marriage, and he certainly hadn't been ready to settle down, no matter what he said. At least she had had sense enough to see that.

She was stowing the last of the sewing supplies and looking forward to changing back into jeans and a sweater when the door to the sunroom opened again and a man entered, obscured from the waist up by a tower of brown boxes. "I met the UPS driver on the way in and he asked me to drop these off," said a deep, velvety voice that sent a hot tremor up Emily's spine and made her wonder if she was hallucinating. "Whoever answered the door told me to bring them back here."

"Thanks." Emily hurried to relieve the man of his burdens, then almost dropped the boxes as she came face-to-face with Brodie Langtry.

The man who had once proposed to her. She felt unsteady on her feet, seeing him here in this house again after so long. And if she was upset, her family was going to be furious.

"Hello, Emily." He grinned, his full lips curving over even, white teeth, eyes sparking with a blatant sex appeal that sent a bolt of remembered heat straight through her. "You're looking well." A single furrow creased his brow. "Though I have to ask—what is that you're wearing?"

She looked down at the prom dress, the hem lopped off and bristling with pins, one ruffle hanging loose where Lacy had started to detach it. She looked back up at Brodie, feeling a little like she had been hit on the head and was still reeling from the blow. "What are you doing here?" she asked.

"As it happens, the Colorado Bureau of Investigation sent me here to help your brother with a case," he said. "I hear you've got a serial murderer problem."

"Does Travis know you're coming?" Her brother

hadn't said anything to her. Then again, he was probably trying to spare her feelings.

"He requested assistance from the CBI, though he doesn't know it's me. Is that going to be a problem?"

She bit her lower lip. "I don't know."

"It's been five years, Emily," he said.

Right. But it might have been five minutes for all the pain that was twisting her stomach. She hadn't expected to react like this. She was supposed to be over Brodie. "You never answered my letter," she said.

The crease across his brow deepened. "You sent me a letter?"

"You mean you don't even remember?" The words came out louder than she had intended, and she forced herself to lower her voice. "I tried calling, but your number had been changed. Travis found out you'd been transferred to Pueblo, so I wrote to you there."

He shook his head. "I never received your letter. Why did you write?"

Did he really not know? She pressed her hand to her stomach, hoping she wasn't going to be sick. This was too awful. "It doesn't matter now." She turned away and tried to make her voice light. "Like you said, it was five years ago. I'm sure Travis will appreciate your help with the case." Her brother was nothing if not a professional.

Brodie was silent, though she could feel his eyes boring into her. She began looking through the stack of packages. "I'll ask again," he said after a moment. "What is that you're wearing?"

"It's a prom dress," she managed.

"Isn't it the wrong time of year for prom? And aren't you in graduate school?"

Her eyes widened and she froze in the act of reaching for a package. "How did you know I'm in graduate school?"

"I might have checked up on you a time or two. They don't have proms in graduate school, do they?"

He'd *checked up* on her. Should she be flattered, or creeped out? "It's the new thing. Haven't you heard?" She continued scanning the labels on the boxes. She picked up the one that surely held her bridesmaid's dress. Maybe instead of stuffing the prom dress back into her closet, she'd burn it at Wednesday night's bonfire. That would be appropriate, wouldn't it?

"What is all this?" Brodie swept his hand to indicate the piles of boxes, bits of tulle, sewing supplies, silk flowers and other flotsam piled around the room. "Are you getting ready for a big party?"

"Travis is getting married on Sunday," Emily said. "I guess you didn't know." Then again, why would he? He and Travis had stopped being friends five years ago.

"No, I didn't know. Good for him. Who's the lucky woman?"

"Her name is Lacy Milligan. I'm sure you don't know her."

"No, but I know of her. Now it's coming back

to me." He grinned. "Lacy is the woman Travis arrested for murder—then after new evidence came to light, he worked to clear her name. I remember the story now, though I didn't know a wedding was in the offing."

It hadn't taken long for the media to latch onto the story of a wrongly accused woman falling in love with the law enforcement officer who had sent her to prison in the first place, then worked to clear her name. Most of the state was probably familiar with the story by now, but Emily didn't want to discuss it with Brodie. "Travis is at his office in town," she said, deciding it was past time to send Brodie on his way. "It's on Main. You can't miss it."

Before he could answer, her cell phone buzzed and she grabbed it off a nearby table. "Hello?"

"Hey." Travis's greeting was casual, but his voice carried the tension that never left him these days. "I was trying to get hold of Lacy, but I can't get through on her phone."

"I think she's talking to Paige, letting her know the highway is open."

"She's terrible about checking her messages, so do me a favor and tell her I'm not going to be able to take her to dinner today. I'm sorry, but we've had a break in the case."

Emily's heart leaped. "Have you made an arrest?"

"Not exactly, but we know who the killers are. One of them is dead, but the other is still on the loose."

"A second murderer?" Travis had long suspected

the Ice Cold Killer might be more than one man. If he had caught one of the killers, surely that meant he was closing in on the second. Maybe the case would be solved before the wedding after all. "Lacy will be glad to hear it," Emily said.

"Maybe not so glad when you tell her I have to miss dinner. I need to focus on tracking down the second man."

Which meant he probably wouldn't be home to sleep, either. "Travis, you can't keep working around the clock like this."

"We're going to get some help. The Colorado Bureau of Investigation has agreed to loan us one of their investigators. Now that the road is open, he— or she—should be showing up anytime."

She glanced over her shoulder at Brodie, who was looking out the window. The past five years had been kind to him, filling out his shoulders, adding a few fine lines around his eyes. He wore his hair a little longer than when she'd last seen him, and sunlight through the window picked out the gold streaks in the brown. Add in chiseled cheekbones, a dimpled chin and a straight nose and it was no wonder he could be mistaken for a model or a movie star.

As if sensing her staring at him, he turned and met her gaze, then cocked one eyebrow, lips half-curved in a mocking smile.

"Emily? Are you still there?" Travis asked.

"Um, your help from the CBI is here," she said. "It's Brodie Langtry." Not waiting to hear Travis's reaction, she thrust the phone at Brodie. *It's Travis*, she mouthed.

Brodie took the phone. "Travis! It's been a long time. I'm looking forward to working with you on this case…Yes, I volunteered for the job. To tell you the truth, I thought it was past time we mended fences. I know we didn't part under the best of circumstances five years ago and I'd like to clear the air. I've been catching up with Emily."

She cringed at the words. She and Brodie didn't need to "catch up." They had had a fun time together once, and if it had ended badly, she took most of the blame for that. She'd been young and naive and had expected things from him that he had never promised to give. She wouldn't make that mistake again.

While he and Travis continued to talk about the case, she turned away and began opening the boxes, enjoying the way the scissors ripped through the tape, letting the sound drown out their conversation. As an investigator with the Colorado Bureau of Investigation, Brodie would no doubt bring a welcome extra pair of eyes to the hunt for the Ice Cold Killer. She needed to remember that he was here to help Travis and probably didn't have the least interest in her. So there was no need for her to feel awkward around him.

Brodie tapped her on the shoulder and held out her phone. "Travis didn't sound very happy to hear from me. Why is that, do you think?"

"You'll have to ask him." But she would make

sure Travis didn't tell Brodie anything he didn't need to know. Best to leave the past in the past.

"I'm going to meet him in town and get caught up on this case," he said. "But I'm hoping to see more of you later."

Before she could think of an answer to this, he leaned forward and kissed her cheek. "It's great to see you again, Emily," he murmured, and she cursed the way her knees wobbled in response.

Then he strode from the room, the door shutting firmly behind him.

Emily groaned and snatched a pillow off the sofa. She hurled it at the door, half wishing Brodie was still standing there and she was aiming at his head. Brodie Langtry was the last person in the world she wanted to see right now. This next week with him was going to be her own version of hell.

Chapter Two

Brodie drove through a world so blindingly white it hurt even with sunglasses shading his eyes. Only the scarred trunks of aspen and the bottle-brush silhouettes of pine trees broke the expanse of glittering porcelain. If not for the walls of plowed snow on either side of the road, it would be difficult in places to distinguish the road from the surrounding fields. After five hours of similar landscape between here and Denver, Emily, in her crazy ruffled pink dress, had stood out like a bird of paradise, a welcome shock to the senses.

Shocking also was how much Travis's little sister had matured. She'd been pretty before—or maybe *cute* was the better word—vivacious and sweet and attractive in a lithe, youthful way. She had filled out since then, her curves more pronounced, her features sharpened into real beauty.

She seemed more serious, but then so was he. Life—and especially a life spent working in law enforcement—did that to people. He'd seen a dark side to people he couldn't forget. It was the kind of thing that left a mark. He couldn't say what had marked Emily, but he saw a new depth and gravity in her expression that hadn't been there before.

He had been such a rascal when they were together five years ago. He had thought Emily was just another fling. He had felt a little guilty about seducing one of his best friend's sisters, but she had been more than willing. And then he had fallen for her—hard. He hadn't been able to imagine a future without her, so he had laid his heart on the line and asked her to spend the rest of her life with him. And she had stomped his heart flat. The memory still hurt. He had offered her everything he had, but that hadn't been enough.

So yeah, that was in the past. He wasn't here to rehash any of it, though he hoped he was man enough to treat her with the respect and kindness she deserved. He owed that to her because she was Travis's sister, and because she had given him some good memories, even if things hadn't worked out.

And now there was this case—a serial killer in Eagle Mountain, of all places. Remote tourist towns weren't the usual hunting grounds for serial killers. They tended to favor big cities, where it was easy to hide and they had a wide choice of prey, or else they moved around a lot, making it tougher for law enforcement to find them. Yet this guy—this Ice Cold Killer—had targeted women in a limited population, during a time when the weather kept him trapped in a small geographic area.

Then again, maybe the killer had taken advantage of the road reopening today and was even now headed out of town.

Brodie steered his Toyota Tundra around an S-curve in the road and had to hit the brakes to avoid rear-ending a vehicle that was half-buried in the plowed snowbank on the right-hand side of the county road. Skid marks on the snow-packed surface of the road told the tale of the driver losing control while rounding the curve and sliding into the drift.

Brodie set his emergency brake, turned on his flashers and hurried out of his vehicle. The car in the snow was a white Jeep Wrangler with Colorado plates. Brodie couldn't see a driver from this angle. Maybe whoever this was had already flagged down another driver and was on the way into town. Boots crunching in the snow, Brodie climbed over a churned-up pile of ice and peered down into the driver's seat.

The woman didn't look like a woman anymore, sprawled across the seat, arms pinned beneath her, blood from the wound at her throat staining the front of her white fur coat. Brodie was reminded of going trapping with an uncle when he was a teenager. They'd come upon a trapped weasel in the snow, its winter-white coat splashed with crimson. Brodie hadn't had the stomach for trapping after that, and he hadn't thought of that moment in twenty years.

Taking a deep, steadying breath, he stepped away from the vehicle and marshaled his composure, then called Travis. "I'm on County Road Seven," he said. "On the way from the ranch into town. I pulled over to check on a car in a ditch. The driver is a woman, her throat's cut. I think we've got another victim."

BRODIE KNEW BETTER than to tell Travis that he looked ten years older since the two had last seen each other. Working a long case would do that to a man, and Travis was the kind who took things to heart more than most. Brodie was here to lift some of that burden. Not everyone liked the CBI interfering with local cases, but Travis had a small department and needed all the help he could get. "It's good to see you again," Brodie said, offering his hand.

Travis ignored the hand and focused on the vehicle in the ditch, avoiding Brodie's gaze. A chill settled somewhere in the pit of Brodie's stomach. So this really was going to be tougher than he had imagined. His old friend resented the way things had ended five years ago. They'd have to clear that up sooner or later, but for now, he'd take his cue from the sheriff and focus on the case.

"I called in the plate number," Brodie said as Travis approached the stranded Jeep. "It's registered to a Jonathan Radford."

Travis nodded. "I know the vehicle. It was stolen two days ago. It was driven by the killers."

"Killers? As in more than one?"

"We've learned the Ice Cold Killer isn't one man, but two. One of them, Tim Dawson, died last night, after kidnapping one of my deputies and her sister. The other—most likely Alex Woodruff—is still at large."

"And still killing." Brodie glanced toward the Jeep. "Most of that blood is still bright red. I think she wasn't killed that long ago."

Travis walked around the Jeep, studying it closely. "Before, Alex and Tim—the killers—always left the victims in their own vehicles."

"Except Fiona Winslow, who was killed at the scavenger hunt on your family's ranch." Brodie had familiarized himself with all the information Travis had sent to the CBI.

"They broke their pattern with Fiona because they were sending a message," Travis said. "Taunting me. I think Alex is doing the same thing with this Jeep. He knows that we know it's the vehicle he was driving until recently."

"Do you think he's driving this woman's car now?" Brodie asked.

Travis shook his head. "That seems too obvious to me, but maybe, if he hasn't found another vehicle. He thinks he's smarter than we are, always one step ahead, but we know who he is now. It won't be as easy to hide. And it will be harder for him to kill alone, too. He's going to make mistakes. I can see it with this woman."

"What do you see?" Reading the case files Travis had emailed was no substitute for eyewitness experience.

"The woman's feet aren't bound. The others were. Maybe that's because he didn't have time, or without Tim's help he couldn't manage it." He moved closer to look into the car once more. "The collar of her fur coat is torn. I think she struggled and tried to fight him off. Maybe she marked him."

"The others didn't have time to put up a fight," Brodie said, recalling the case notes.

Travis opened the door and leaned into the car, being careful not to touch anything. With gloved hands, he felt gingerly around the edge of the seat and along the dash. When he withdrew and straightened, he held a small rectangle of card stock in his hand, the words *ICE COLD* printed across the front. "He's following his pattern of leaving the card," Brodie said.

"He doesn't want there to be any doubt about who's responsible," Travis said. He pulled out an evidence envelope and sealed the card inside. "It's another way to thumb his nose at us."

They turned at the sound of an approaching vehicle, or rather, a caravan of two sheriff's department SUVs and a black Jeep, traveling slowly up the snow-packed road. The vehicles parked on the opposite side of the road and two deputies and an older man bundled in a heavy coat got out.

"Hello, Gage," Brodie greeted one of the deputies, Travis's brother, Gage Walker.

"You're about the last person I expected to see here," Gage said. He seemed puzzled, but not unfriendly, and, unlike his brother, was willing to shake Brodie's hand. "Typical of CBI to show up when we have the case half-solved."

"Dwight Prentice." The second deputy, a tall, rangy blond, offered his hand and Brodie shook it.

"And this is Butch Collins, the county medical examiner." Travis introduced the older man, who nodded and moved on to the car. His face paled when he looked into the vehicle.

"Something wrong?" Travis asked, hurrying to the older man's side.

Collins shook his head. "I know her, that's all." He cleared his throat. "Lynn Wallace. She sings in the choir at my church."

"Do you know what kind of car she drives?" Brodie asked, joining them.

Collins stared at him, then back at the Jeep. "This isn't her car?"

"It was stolen from a local vacation home two days ago," Travis said. "We think the killer might have been driving it."

"I don't know what kind of car Lynn drove," Collins said. "Only that she was a lovely woman with a beautiful soprano voice. She didn't deserve this. But then, none of them did." He straightened his shoulders. "Are you ready for me to look at her?"

"Give us a few seconds to process the outside of the car, then you can have a look." Travis motioned to Gage and Dwight, who moved forward.

Travis indicated Brodie should follow him. "I need you to get to work on identifying Lynn Wallace's vehicle," he said. "I think Alex will ditch it as soon as he can, but he might not have had a chance yet. You can use my office."

"Tell me what you know about Alex," Brodie said.

"Alex Woodruff. A college student at the Colorado State University—or he was until recently. He doesn't have any priors, at least under that name, and that's the only name I've found for him."

"Emily goes to the Colorado State University, doesn't she?" Brodie asked. Knowing he was coming to Eagle Mountain, he'd checked her Facebook page. "Do they know each other?"

The lines around Travis's mouth tightened. "She says he participated in a research study she and her colleagues conducted, but they weren't friends, just acquaintances."

"What brought him to Eagle Mountain?"

"He and Tim supposedly came here to ice climb over their winter break and got stuck here when blizzards closed the highway. They were staying at an aunt's vacation cabin until recently."

"I'll get right on the search for the car," Brodie said. As he walked to his SUV, he considered the connection between Alex Woodruff and Emily Walker. His work investigating crimes had taught him to be skeptical of coincidence, but until he had further proof, he wasn't going to add to Travis's concerns by voicing the worry that now filled his mind. What if the thing that had brought Alex and Tim to Eagle Mountain wasn't ice climbing—but Emily?

Chapter Three

"Thank you, Professor. That would be so helpful. I'll review everything and be ready to discuss it when I see you next week after the wedding." Emily hung up the phone and mentally checked off one more item on her Tuesday to-do list. All her professors had agreed to excuse her for another week so that she could help with the preparations for Travis and Lacy's wedding. Though she could have made the six-hour drive back to Fort Collins to attend a few classes and try to catch up on all she had missed while stranded by the snow, the last thing she wanted was for the road to close again, forcing her to miss the wedding.

Instead, someone in her department had volunteered to make the drive out here to deliver files for Emily to review. She had protested that it was ridiculous to make such a long drive, but apparently more than one person had been eager for the excuse to get off campus for a while. The risk of getting stranded in Eagle Mountain if another storm system rolled in had only heightened the appeal.

She moved on to the next item on her list. She needed to check on her horse, Witchy. The mare had developed inflammation in one leg shortly after the first of the year and veterinarian Darcy Marsh had prescribed a course of treatment that appeared to be working, but Emily was supposed to exercise her lightly each day and check that there was no new swelling. Slipping on her barn coat—the same one she had worn as a teenager—she headed out the door and down the drive to the horse barn. Sunlight shimmered on the snow that covered everything like a starched white sheet. Every breath stung her nose, reminding her that temperatures hovered in the twenties. She still marveled that it could be so cold when the sun shone so brightly overhead, giving the air a clean, lemony light.

The barn's interior presented a sharp contrast to the outside world, its atmosphere warm from the breath of animals and smelling of a not-unpleasant mixture of molasses, hay and manure. A plaintive *meow!* greeted Emily, and a gray-striped cat trotted toward her, the cat's belly swollen with kittens soon to be born. "Aww, Tawny." Emily bent and gently stroked the cat, who started up a rumbling purr and leaned against Emily's legs. "It won't be long now, will it?" Emily crooned, feeling the kittens shift beneath her hand. She'd have to make sure Tawny had a warm, comfortable place to give birth.

She straightened and several of the family's horses poked their heads over the tops of their stalls. Witchy, in an end stall on the left-hand side, whinnied softly and stamped against the concrete floor of her stall.

Emily slipped into the stall and greeted Witchy, patting her neck, then bent to examine the bandaged front pastern. It no longer felt hot or swollen, though Darcy had recommended wrapping it for a few weeks longer to provide extra support. Emily breathed a sigh of relief. For a brief period during her childhood, she had considered studying to be a veterinarian, but had quickly ruled out any job that required dealing with animals' suffering.

"Are you contemplating climbing down out of your ivory tower and hiring on as the newest ranch hand?"

Emily froze as Brodie's oh-so-familiar teasing tone and velvety voice flowed around her like salted caramel—both sweet and biting. She was aware of her position, bent over with her backside facing the stall door, where she sensed him standing. She turned her head, and sure enough, Brodie had leaned over the top half of the stall door, grinning, the cat cradled in his arms.

With as much dignity as she could muster, she released her hold on the horse's leg and straightened. "Brodie, what are you doing here?" she asked.

He stroked the cat under the chin. Tawny closed her eyes and purred even louder. Emily had an uncomfortable memory of Brodie stroking *her*— eliciting a response not unlike that of the cat. "I was looking for you," he said. "Someone told me you're in charge of a bonfire and barbecue here Wednesday."

"Yes." She took a lead rope from a peg just outside the stall door and clipped it onto Witchy's halter. The mare regarded her with big gold-brown eyes like warm honey. "What about it?"

"I was hoping to wrangle an invite, since I'm staying on the ranch. It would be awkward if I felt the need to lock myself in my cabin for the evening."

She slid back the latch on the door and pushed it open, forcing Brodie to stand aside, then led the mare out. "I have to exercise Witchy," she said.

He gave the cat a last pat, then set her gently aside and fell into step beside Emily, matching his long strides to her own shorter ones. "I didn't realize you were staying at the ranch," she said. He hadn't been at dinner last night, but then, neither had Travis. The two men had been working on the case. Frankly, she was shocked her parents had invited Brodie to stay. They certainly had no love lost for him, after what had happened between him and Emily.

"When the CBI agreed to send an investigator to help with the Ice Cold Killer case, Travis asked your parents if they could provide a place for the officer to stay. They were kind enough to offer up one of their guest cabins."

"Wouldn't it be more convenient for you in town?" she asked.

"There aren't any rooms in town," Brodie said. "They're all full of people stranded here by the road closure. I imagine that will change now that the av-alanches have been cleared and it's safe to travel again, but in the meantime, your folks were gracious enough to let me stay." He fell silent, but she could feel his eyes on her, heating her neck and sending prickles of awareness along her arms. "Does it bother you, having me here?" he asked.

"Of course not."

She led Witchy out of the barn, along a fenced passage to a covered arena. Brodie moved forward to open the gate for her. "Are you going to ride her?" he asked.

Emily shook her head. "She's still recovering from an injury. But I need to walk her around the arena for a few laps."

"I'll walk with you." He didn't bother asking permission—men like Brodie didn't ask. He wasn't cruel or demanding or even particularly arrogant. He just accepted what people—women—had always given him—attention, time, sex. All he had to do was smile and flash those sea-blue eyes and most women would give him anything he wanted.

She had been like that, too, so she understood the magnetism of the man. But she wasn't that adoring girl anymore, and she knew to be wary. "Of course you can come to the bonfire," she said. "It's really no big deal."

She began leading the mare around the arena, watching the horse for any sign of pain or weakness, but very aware of the man beside her. "Tell me about Alex Woodruff," he said.

The question startled her, so much that she stumbled. She caught herself and continued on as if nothing had happened. "Why are you asking me about Alex?"

"I've been reviewing all the case notes. He was here, at the scavenger hunt the day Fiona Winslow was killed."

"Yes. He and his friend Tim were here. I invited them."

"Why did you do that?"

"I knew the road closure had stranded them here and I felt sorry for them, stuck in a small town where they didn't know many people. I figured the party would be something fun for them to do, and a way to meet some local people near their age." She cut her gaze over to him. "Why are you asking me about Alex?"

He did that annoying thing Travis sometimes did, answering a question with a question. "You knew Alex and Tim from the university?"

"I didn't really know them." She stopped and bent to run her hand down Witchy's leg, feeling for any warmth or swelling or sign of inflammation. "They both signed up as volunteers for research we were doing. Lots of students do. Most of the studies only pay five to ten dollars, but the work isn't hard and cash is cash to a broke student."

"What kind of research?" Brodie asked.

She straightened and looked him in the eye. She loved her work and could talk about it with almost anyone. If she talked long enough, maybe he'd get bored and leave. "I'm studying behavioral economics. It's sort of a melding of traditional psychology and economics. We look at how people make the buying decisions they make and why. Almost every choice has a price attached to it, and it can be interesting what motivates people to act one way versus another."

"How did Alex and Tim hear about your experiments?"

"We have flyers all over campus, and on social media." She shrugged. "They were both psychology majors, so I think the research appealed to them. I ran into Alex in a coffee shop on campus two days later and he had a lot of intelligent questions about what we were doing."

"Maybe he had studied so he'd have questions prepared so he could keep you talking," Brodie said. "Maybe he was flirting with you."

"Oh, please." She didn't hide her scorn for this idea. "He was not flirting. If anything, he was showing off."

One eyebrow rose a scant quarter inch—enough to make him look even cockier than usual. "Showing off is some men's idea of flirting."

"You would know about that, wouldn't you?"

His wicked grin sent a current of heat through her. "When you're good, it's not showing off," he said.

She wished she was the kind of woman who had a snappy comeback for a line like that, but it was taking all her concentration to avoid letting him see he was getting to her. So instead of continuing to flirt, she started forward with the horse once more and changed the subject. "Are you going to be able to help Travis catch the Ice Cold Killer?" she asked.

Brodie's expression sobered. Yes, nothing like a serial murderer to dampen the libido. "I'm going to do my best," he said. "We know who we're looking for now—we just have to find him."

She managed not to stumble this time, but she did turn to look at him. "You know who the killer is?"

He frowned. "Travis didn't tell you?"

"I haven't seen Travis in several days. He's either working or spending time with Lacy. He told me on the phone that one of the men he thought was involved is dead, but that there was another one he was after."

Brodie said nothing.

She stopped and faced him. "Tell me who it is," she said. "You know I won't go talking to the press."

"The man who died was Tim Dawson," Brodie said.

All the breath went out of her as this news registered. "Then the other man is Alex Woodruff." She grabbed his arm. "That's why you were asking me about him. But he and Tim left town when the road opened briefly a couple of weeks ago. Travis said so."

"They moved out of the cabin where they were

staying, but now Travis believes they stayed in the area. If you have any idea where Alex might be hiding, or what he's likely to do next, you need to tell me." She released her hold on him and stepped back, the mare's warm bulk reassuring. If her suddenly weak legs gave out, she'd have the animal to grab on to. "I hardly know him," she said. "But a serial killer? Why would a smart, good-looking guy from a well-off family want to murder a bunch of women he doesn't even know?" And how could she have spent time with Alex and Tim and not seen that kind of evil in them?

"You're more likely to have an answer for that than I do," Brodie said. "You're conducting a lot of research on human behavior and motivation. Didn't you do one study on what motivates people to break rules or to cheat?"

"What did you do—run a background check on me? That's creepy."

"All I did was look at your public Facebook page," he said. "And there's nothing creepy about it. I knew I was coming here and I wanted to see how you were doing—as a friend. I guess you never did the same for me."

She couldn't keep color from flooding her cheeks. She had, in fact, perused Brodie's Facebook page more than once, as well as Googling his name for tidbits of information. Not because she still felt anything for him, simply because she was curious. "All right," she said. "As long as you're not being a creep."

"Such technical language from a psychologist."

"Behavioral economics is different," she said. "There's psychology involved, of course, but nothing that would give me insight into the mind of a serial killer."

"I think you're wrong," he said. "I think you probably can tell us things we don't know about Alex Woodruff. You've always been smart about people."

I wasn't smart about you. She bit her lip to hold back the words. "I'm sure the CBI has profilers who specialize in this kind of thing," she said.

"Yes, but they don't know Alex, and they don't know Eagle Mountain. You do."

She searched his face, trying to read his expression. He was focused on her in that intense way he had—a way that made her feel like she was the only person in the world he wanted to be with right this second. "What do you want from me?" she asked.

"I want you to think about Alex, and about this area, and see if you can come up with any ideas that might help us."

She shook her head. "I think you're grasping at straws. You need to consult a professional."

"We will. You're just another avenue for us to explore. You never know in a case like this what might be the key to a solution."

"Does Travis know you're asking me to help?"

"No, but I can't see why he'd object. I'm not asking you to do anything dangerous."

She nodded. "All right. I don't think it will do

any good, but I'll think about it and see what I can come up with."

He clapped her on the shoulder. "Thanks. I knew I could count on you."

How had he known he could count on her? But she couldn't ask the question. He was already striding out of the arena, his boots making neat prints in the raked dirt.

Brodie had to know she would do anything to help her brother. If Travis had asked her for help with the case, she wouldn't have hesitated. That she was less willing to cooperate with Brodie probably said more about her feelings for him than she cared to admit.

Never mind. She would try to come up with some ideas about Alex and—with her help or not—Travis and Brodie would catch him and put him in jail for a long time.

Then she could go back to her normal life, with no serial killers—and no former lovers—to unsettle her.

"YOUR SISTER HAS agreed to serve as a consultant on the case."

Travis was so even-keeled and unemotional that Brodie considered it a personal challenge to attempt to get a reaction from him. He'd scored a hit with this announcement.

Travis looked up from the file he'd been studying, eyes sparking with annoyance. "What could Emily possibly contribute to the case?" he asked.

Brodie moved out of the doorway where he'd been

standing and dropped into one of the two chairs in front of Travis's desk. The small office was spartan in appearance, with only a laptop and an inch-high stack of papers on Travis's desk, and a few family photographs and citations on the walls. Brodie's own desk at CBI headquarters in Denver was crammed with so many books, files and photographs his co-workers had hinted that it might be a fire hazard. But hey, the clutter worked for him. "Emily knows Alex Woodruff and she's studied psychology," he said. "She can give us insights into his character and what he's likely to do next."

"She's an economics major—not a profiler."

"We'll still consult the CBI profiler," Brodie said. "But I think Emily will come to this with fresh eyes. Besides, she knows this county almost as well as you do. She might be able to give us some new ideas about places to look for him."

Travis shook his head. "He's probably left the county by now. The highway is open, and he has to know we're on his trail. A smart man would be half-way to Mexico by now."

"You and I both know criminals rarely behave the way most people would. Alex may be smart, but he's arrogant, too. He's been taunting you, leaving those business cards, killing a woman on your family ranch, going after one of your deputies. He still thinks he can beat you."

"Maybe." Travis fixed Brodie with a stare that had probably caused more than one felon to shake in his shoes. "This isn't some scheme you've come up with in order for you to spend more time with Emily, is it?" he asked. "Because I'm not going to stand by and let that happen again."

"Let what happen?" Brodie had a strong sense of déjà vu. He recalled another conversation with Travis that had begun like this, five years ago, when his friend—only a deputy then—had accused him of trying to seduce Emily.

"Emily really hurt when the two of you broke things off," Travis said. "It took a long time for her to get over you. I don't want her to have to go through that again."

Brodie bristled. "She's the one who ended it, not me."

"You must have had something to do with it."

Brodie ground his teeth together. He did not want to argue about this with Travis. "I didn't come here to get back together with your sister," he said. "I came to help with this case. I asked Emily to consult because I think she's another resource we can draw on."

Travis uncrossed his arms, and the tension around his mouth eased. "Fair enough. I won't rule out anything that might help us catch Alex Woodruff. Speaking of that, have you had any luck tracking down Lynn Wallace's car?"

"Not yet. She drove a white Volvo." Brodie opened his phone and read the license plate number from his notes. "Nothing flashy. Fairly common. Easy to hide."

"Right. I'll put my deputies on the lookout." He turned to a map pinned to the wall of his office. Pins showed the locations where each of the Ice Cold Killer's seven victims had been found. "Alex and Tim working together concentrated the murders in three areas," he said. "Christy O'Brien and Anita Allbritton were killed within Eagle Mountain town limits. Kelly Farrow and Michaela Underwood were both murdered in the area around Dixon Pass and the national forest service land near there. Fiona Winslow, Lauren Grenado and Lynn Wallace were all killed within a couple of miles of the Walking W ranch." Travis indicated a third grouping of pins on the map.

"Does that tell us anything about where Alex might be hiding now?" Brodie asked.

Travis pointed to a red pin on County Road Five. "We know Tim and Alex were staying at Tim's aunt's cabin, here, when the first three murders took place. They spent some time in a vacation home here." He indicated another pin. "And they may have been at this summer cabin in the national forest, here, for the other murders. Now—who knows?"

A tapping on the door frame interrupted them. Both men turned to see office manager Adelaide Kinkaid, a sixtysomething woman who wore what looked like red monkeys dangling from her earlobes, and a flowing red-and-purple tunic over black slacks. "We just got word that a fresh slide on Dixon Pass sent one vehicle over the edge and buried two others," she said. "Fortunately, they were able to dig everyone out pretty quickly, but the road is closed until they can clear up the mess."

Brodie groaned. "How many delivery trucks do you suppose got caught on the wrong side of this one?" he asked.

"Probably about as many as were able to leave town when the road opened," Adelaide said. "Everyone is just trading places."

"I'll take your word for it," Brodie said. "You do seem to know everything." He leaned toward her. "Are those monkey earrings?"

"Yes." She tapped one earring with a red-painted fingernail. "Do you like them?"

"Only you could pull off a look like that, Adelaide," Brodie said, grinning.

She swatted his shoulder. "You're the kind of man I always warned my daughters about."

"What kind is that?"

"Too smart and good-looking for your own good. The kind of man who's oblivious to the broken hearts he leaves behind."

"Adelaide, Brodie is here as a fellow law enforcement officer," Travis said. "He deserves our respect."

"I'm sure he's a sterling officer," Adelaide said. "And a fine man all around. Just not marriage material—which is probably okay with him." She grinned, then turned to Travis. "And speaking of marriages, don't you have a tux fitting to see to?"

Color rose in the sheriff's cheeks. "I don't need

you to keep track of my schedule, Addie," he said. "Right now I have a case to work on."

"You always have a case to work on," Adelaide said. "You only have one wedding." She whirled and stalked away.

Brodie settled back in his chair once more. "Do you have a tux fitting?" he asked.

"I canceled it."

"Unless you're going to get married in your uniform, are you sure that's a good idea?"

Travis scowled at Brodie. "They have my measurements. They don't need me." His phone rang and he answered it. "Hello?"

He listened for a moment, then said, "I've got Brodie in the office. I'm going to put you on speaker." He punched the keypad. "All right. Say that again."

"I've got what looks like another victim of the Ice Cold Killer," Deputy Dwight Prentice said. "Taped up, throat cut, left in her car near the top of Dixon Pass. Only, she's still alive. The ambulance is on its way."

Travis was already standing. "So are we," he said.

Chapter Four

The woman—a once-pretty brunette, her skin bleached of color and her hair matted with blood—stared up at them, glassy-eyed, her lips moving, but no sound coming out. "You're safe now," Brodie said, leaning over her. "We're going to take care of you." He stepped back as the EMTs moved in to transfer the woman to a waiting gurney.

"We've already called for a helicopter," the older of the two paramedics said. "I think this is more than the clinic in Eagle Mountain can handle. They've agreed to meet us at the ball fields, where it's open enough for them to land."

Brodie's gaze shifted to the woman again. She had closed her eyes and her breath came in ragged gasps. He wanted to grab her hand and encourage her to hang on, but he needed to move out of the way and let the paramedics do their job.

Travis, who had been talking to Dwight and highway patrolman Ryder Stewart, motioned for Brodie to join them. "Her name is Denise Switcher," Ryder said. "We found her driver's license in the purse on the passenger floorboard, and the registration on the car matches. Her address is in Fort Collins."

"Did she say anything about what happened?" Brodie asked.

"I don't think she can talk," Dwight said. "One of the EMTs said the vocal chords may be damaged."

Brodie winced. "How is it she's still alive?"

"I don't know," Travis said. "But I hope she stays that way." He nodded to Dwight. "You must have come along right after it happened. Did you see anything or anyone who might have been Alex?"

"No." Dwight hooked his thumbs over his utility belt and stared toward the EMTs bent over the woman. "A trucker who was pulled over taking off his tire chains flagged me down and said he spotted a car on the side of the road near the top of the pass. He didn't see anyone in it, but thought maybe I'd want to check." Dwight pulled a notebook from inside his leather coat. "Gary Ellicott. He was delivering groceries to Eagle Mountain and somehow missed that the road had been closed again. When he got to the barricades, he had to back down a ways before he could turn around. He thinks about fifteen minutes had passed between the time he spotted the car and when he talked to me."

"I don't think she was lying there very long," Brodie said. "A wound like that bleeds fast." If much more time had passed, she would have bled to death.

"The road closed seventy-five minutes ago,"

Ryder said. "There was a lot of traffic up here and it took maybe half an hour to clear out. If the killer was cutting her throat then, someone would have seen."

"So this most likely happened between thirty and forty-five minutes ago," Brodie said.

"But he would have had to have stopped the car before the road closed," Travis said. "The car is on the southbound side of the road, headed toward town. That seems to indicate she was arriving, not leaving."

"We'll need to find out if she was staying in town," Brodie said. "Maybe she has family in Eagle Mountain, was leaving and, like the truck driver, had to turn around because of the barricade."

"If this is Alex's work and not a copycat, that means he didn't leave town," Travis said.

The paramedics shut the door of the ambulance and hurried to the cab. Siren wailing, they pulled away, headed back toward town. "Let's take a look," Travis said, and led the way to the car, a gray Nissan sedan with Colorado plates. It was parked up against a six-foot berm of plowed snow, so close it was impossible to open the passenger side door. The snow around the vehicle had been churned by the footsteps of the paramedics and cops, to the point that no one shoe impression was discernable. "I took photographs of the scene before I approached," Dwight said. "But I can tell you there weren't any footprints. If I had to guess, I'd say the killer used a rake or shovel to literally cover his tracks."

Brodie continued to study the roadside. "I don't see any other tire impressions," he said.

"He could have parked on the pavement," Ryder said.

"Or he could have been on foot," Travis said.

"It's four miles from town up a half-dozen switchbacks," Ryder said. "That's a long way to walk. Someone would have noticed."

"Not if he stayed behind the snow." Travis kicked steps into the snowbank and scrambled to the top and looked down. "There's a kind of path stomped out over here."

Brodie climbed up beside him and stared down at the narrow trail. "It might be an animal trail."

"It might be. Or it could be how Alex made his way up to this point without being seen. Then he stepped out in the road and flagged down Denise and pretended to be a stranded motorist."

"How did he know the driver was a woman by herself?" Brodie asked.

"He could have studied approaching traffic with binoculars."

The two men descended once more to the others beside the car. "Why would any woman stop for him, knowing there's a killer on the loose?" Dwight asked.

"She was from Fort Collins," Travis said. "I don't know how much press these murders have been getting over there. It wouldn't be front-page news or the top story on a newscast."

"He's right," Brodie said. "I've seen a few articles in the Denver papers, but not much. It would be easy to miss."

"Alex is a good-looking young man," Travis said. "Clean-cut, well dressed. If he presented himself as a stranded motorist, stuck in the cold far from town, most people would be sympathetic."

"Maybe he dressed as a woman, the way Tim did when they were working together," Dwight said. "People would be even more likely to stop for a woman."

"Alex and Tim were both amateur actors, right?" Brodie asked, trying to recall information from the reports he had read.

"Yeah," Ryder said. "And we know that, at least a few times, Tim dressed as a woman who was trying to escape an abusive boyfriend or husband. He flagged down another woman and asked for help, then Alex moved in to attack. One woman was able to escape and described the scenario for us."

Travis pulled on a pair of gloves, then opened the driver's-side door. He leaned in and came out with a woman's purse—black leather with a gold clasp. He pulled out the wallet and scanned the ID, then flipped through the credit cards until he came to a slim white card with an embossed photograph of a smiling brunette—Denise Switcher. "Looks like she worked at Colorado State University," he said.

The hair rose on the back of Brodie's neck. "Emily's school," he said. He didn't like another connection to Emily in this case.

"Alex's school." Travis slid the card back into the wallet. "I wonder if he chose her because he recognized her."

"That might have made her more likely to stop to help him out," Dwight said.

Travis returned the wallet to the purse and rifled through the rest of the contents. Expression grim, he pulled out a white business card, the words *ICE COLD* in black ink printed on one side.

The card taunted them—a reminder that, yes, they knew who attacked Denise Switcher, but they weren't any closer to catching him than they had ever been.

They were still silently contemplating the card when Travis's phone rang. He listened for a moment, then ended the call. "That was one of the paramedics," he said. "Denise Switcher coded before Flight for Life arrived. She's dead."

Brodie silently cursed the waste of a young woman's life, as well as their best chance to learn more about Alex's methods and motives. He turned to walk back toward the sheriff's department vehicle, but drew up short as a red Jeep skidded to a stop inches in front of him. The driver's door flew open and Emily stumbled out. "Is it true? Did the killer really get Denise?" she demanded, looking wildly around.

Brodie hurried to her. She wore only leggings and a thin sweater and tennis shoes, and was already shivering in the biting cold. He shrugged out of his jacket. "What are you doing here?" he asked.

She waved off his attempts to put his jacket around her. "You have to tell me. That ambulance I passed—was it Denise? Does that mean she's still alive?"

Travis joined them. "Emily, you shouldn't be here," he said.

"I was in the Cake Walk Café, waiting. Then Tammy Patterson came in and said she heard from a source at the sheriff's department that the Ice Cold Killer had attacked another woman. I had the most awful feeling it was Denise." She bit her bottom lip, her eyes fixed on Travis, her expression pleading.

He put a hand on her shoulder. "It was Denise Switcher," he said. "But how did you know?"

"Tammy said the woman was from Fort Collins. I was hoping that was just a coincidence, but…" She buried her face against Travis's shoulder.

"Emily?" Brodie approached, his voice gentle. "What was Denise doing in Eagle Mountain?"

She raised her head and wiped away tears. "I'm sorry. I thought I said. She was coming to see me."

BRODIE WORE WHAT Emily thought of as his cop face—grim determination and what felt like censure, as if he suspected her of withholding important information. She refused to give in to the temptation to cower against Travis, so she straightened and wiped the tears from her eyes.

Brodie, still scowling, thrust his jacket at her once more. "Put this on. You're freezing."

She would have liked nothing better than to re-fuse the offer, but the truth was, she was so cold she couldn't stop shaking. She'd been so upset she had left her own coat behind at the café. She mutely accepted his jacket and slipped into it, his warmth enveloping her, along with the scent of him, clean and masculine.

"Why was Denise coming to see you?" Travis asked.

"The lead on the research project I'm involved in had some files he wanted me to review," she said. "Denise volunteered to deliver them to me."

"She drove six hours to deliver files?" Brodie asked. "Why didn't they transmit them electronically? Or ask you to make the trip?"

"These are paper surveys students filled out," she said. "And the professor had already agreed I should stay here in Eagle Mountain until after the wedding." She hugged the coat more tightly around her. "Honestly, I don't think he would have bothered, except Denise wanted to come. She said it was a great excuse to get out of the office and spend at least one night in the mountains."

"The two of you were friends?" Travis asked.

She nodded, and bit the inside of her cheek to stave off the fresh wave of tears that threatened with that one change of verb tense—*were*. "She's the ad-ministrative assistant in the economics department and she and I really hit it off. I'd told her so much about Eagle Mountain and the ranch that she was anxious to see it." She swallowed hard. If Denise had stayed in Fort Collins, she'd be alive now.

"When did you talk to her last?" Travis asked.

"She called me when she stopped for gas in Gunnison, and we agreed to meet at the Cake Walk for lunch."

"What time was that?" Brodie asked.

"About ten thirty."

"Did Alex Woodruff know her?" Brodie asked.

Had Denise known her killer? Emily shuddered at the thought, then forced herself to focus on the question. "Maybe," she said. "Students can register online to participate in various research studies, but they can also come into the office and fill out the paperwork there. If Alex did that, he would have met Denise. And a couple of times she's helped check people in for studies."

"So there's a good chance he did know her," Brodie said.

"Yes." She glanced toward the gray Nissan. "What happened to her? I mean, I know she was killed, but why up here?"

"It's possible Alex posed as a stranded motorist in need of a ride," Travis said. "If your friend recognized him from school, do you think she would have stopped?"

Emily nodded. "Yes. Denise was always pitching in to help with fund-raisers or any extra work that needed to be done. She would have stopped to help someone, especially someone she knew." Again, she struggled for composure. "I'm sure she has family in Denver. Someone will have to tell them."

"I'll take care of that," Travis said.

She wanted to hug her brother. He had had to break the awful news to too many parents and spouses and siblings since the killings had begun. "Why is Alex doing this?" she asked.

"We're hoping you can give us some insight into that," Brodie said. "You might talk to some of the professors who knew him. We could call them, but they might be more inclined to open up to you. You're one of them."

"What is that supposed to mean?" she asked.

"You're an academic," he said. "You speak their language. I'm just a dumb cop."

Under other circumstances, she might have laughed. Brodie was anything but dumb. But there was nothing funny about what had happened here today. "I'll see what I can find out," she said. "But I'm not promising I can help you."

"We'd appreciate it if you'd try." Travis patted her shoulder. "I'm sorry about your friend, but I think you'd better go home now. There's nothing you can do here."

She nodded, and slipped off the jacket and held it out to Brodie. "You keep it," he said. "I can get it tonight."

"Don't be silly," she said. "I'm getting back in my warm car, so I don't need it." And she didn't want to give him an excuse for looking her up again later.

He took the jacket, then turned toward her Jeep, frowning. "You drove up here by yourself?" he said.

"Yes."

"You shouldn't be out driving by yourself," he said. "Alex Woodruff targets women who are in their cars alone."

"I'm not going to stop if he tries to flag me down," she said. "I'm not stupid."

"He knows that," Brodie said. "He would use some subterfuge. He's done it before."

"Brodie's right," Travis said. "From now on, when you have to come to town, take someone else with you. And don't pull over for anyone—no matter what."

She stared at them, fear tightening her throat and making it hard to breathe. Of course she knew there was a killer preying on women. But it was hard to believe she was really in danger. That was probably what those other women had thought, too. She nodded. "All right," she said. "I won't go out alone, and I'll be careful."

Brodie followed her to the Jeep and waited while she climbed in. "I know you think Travis and I are overreacting," he said. "But until this man is caught, you're not going to be truly safe."

"I know." She didn't like knowing it, but there was no use denying facts. For whatever reason, Alex Woodruff was targeting women who were alone—women in her age group. "I do take this very seriously," she said. Having a brother who was sheriff and another brother who was a deputy didn't make her immune from the danger.

Chapter Five

Emily couldn't shake a sense of guilt over Denise's death. She could have refused her friend's offer to bring the student surveys to her. She could have at least warned Denise to be careful, and made sure she knew about the serial killer who had been targeting women in the area. But she couldn't change the past, and guilt wouldn't bring Denise back to her. All Emily could do was to try to help Travis and his officers find Alex and stop him before he killed again.

With this in mind, she called the professor who had taught several of the undergrad psychology courses she had taken at the university. "It's always wonderful to hear from a former student," Professor Brandt said, after Emily had introduced herself. "Even if you did forsake psychology for economics."

"I still have one foot in the psychology camp," she said. "And I use things you taught me almost every day."

Professor Brandt laughed. "You must want a big

favor indeed if you're ladling out flattery like that," he said. "What can I do for you?"

"I'm calling about an undergrad, a psychology major who participated in some research I'm conducting," she said. "I need to get in touch with him, but I'm not having any luck. I'm wondering if you know how to reach him. His name is Alex Woodruff."

"Yes, I have had Alex in several classes," the professor said. "He was enrolled in my experimental psychology course this semester, but my understanding is that he never reported for classes."

"Do you know why?" she asked. "Has he been in touch with you?"

"No. There are always a number of students who drop out each semester for various reasons."

"Do you have any idea where he might be? Did he mention moving or anything like that?"

"No. But then, I doubt he would have confided in me. He wasn't the type to seek out faculty for conversation."

"What type was he?" Emily asked. "What were your impressions of him?"

"He was intelligent, good-looking. A bit arrogant. The type of student who doesn't have to work very hard or put forth much effort to get good grades. If I had to describe him in one word, I'd say he was superficial."

"Superficial?" she repeated. "What do you mean?"

"He was chameleonlike, adjusting himself to his

circumstances. He could play the part of the studious scholar or the popular jock, but I always had the impression they were all just roles for him. Watching him was like watching an actor in a play. I never had a sense that he ever really revealed anything about himself."

"Yes, I saw that, too," Emily said, a chill shuddering up her spine. When she had met Alex, he had played the role of the eager research participant, an average student earning a little pocket change, no different from the majority of other students who filled out her questionnaires. But chances were his fantasies of murdering women had been well formed by then. The literature she had read about serial killers pointed to their compulsions building from a young age.

"I do remember one time the subject of future professions came up in class, and Alex said he wanted to go into law enforcement. He specifically mentioned becoming a profiler."

Another shudder went through her. "Did that strike you as odd?" she asked.

"Not really. Television has made the profession glamorous. I always point out to students that they'll need experience in some other branch of psychology before they can make the leap to criminal profiling."

"Did Alex have any particular friends at the university?" she asked. "A girlfriend?"

"I don't know," the professor said. "Why your interest in Alex? If you're unable to follow up with him, you can always discard his responses from your research."

"It seems odd to me that such a promising student would suddenly drop out of school," she said, grappling for some plausible explanation for her interest. "I know it's none of my business, but someone must know something. I guess I hate leaving a mystery unsolved."

"Now you've got me curious," he said. "I tell you what—I'll ask around a little and see what I can find out. Is this a good number for you?"

"Yes. I'm staying with my parents for my brother's wedding this weekend. I appreciate anything you can find out."

"I'll talk to you soon, then."

She ended the call and stared out the window at the snow-covered landscape. What role was Alex playing today? Was he safe and warm in the home of an unsuspecting friend, or hunkered down in a cave or a remote cabin, preparing to kill again? Why hadn't she—or the other people who knew him— seen in him the capacity to murder? Was it because he hid that side of himself so well—or because as humans they shied away from admitting the possibility that such evil lay in someone who was, after all, so very much like themselves?

BRODIE HAD NEVER thought of Emily as a serious person. He had a fixed image of her as young, fun and carefree. But maybe that was only because they had been like that when they had been a couple five years before. Time and the job had made him more somber, and he could see that in her also. He stood in the doorway of the sunroom that evening, studying her as she sat on a love seat across the room: legs curled under her, head bent over a thick textbook, dark hair in a knot on top of her head, brows drawn together in concentration. Travis's words to him earlier still stung—had she really been so hurt by their breakup? It had been what she wanted, wasn't it—to be rid of a man she couldn't see herself with permanently?

She looked up from the book and noticed him. "How long have you been standing there?" she asked.

"Not long." He moved into the room and held out the stack of file folders he had tucked under his arm. "I retrieved these from Denise Switcher's car. I think they're the files you said she was bringing to you." The box the files had been packed in had been spattered with blood, so he had removed them. No need to remind Emily of the violent way her friend had died.

She hesitated, then reached up to take the folders. "Thank you."

When he didn't leave, but stood in front of her, hands tucked in the pockets of his jeans, she motioned to the love seat across from her. "Do you want to sit down?"

He sat. "Are you okay?" he asked.

"Why wouldn't I be okay?" She pulled a pencil from the back of her head and her hair tumbled down around her shoulders. He'd always wondered how women did that—styled their hair with a pencil or a chopstick or whatever was handy.

"It's hard, losing a friend to murder," he said.

She nodded. "It's worse knowing someone you knew killed her." She shifted, planting her feet on the floor. "Did you have something to eat? I think Rainey kept back some dinner for you and Travis."

"I'll get it in a minute."

He let the silence stretch. It was a good technique for getting people to open up. He used it in interrogating suspects—though he wasn't interrogating Emily, and he didn't suspect her of anything more than being uncomfortable around him. He'd like to change that.

"I talked to one of Alex's professors," she said after a moment. She glanced at him through a veil of dark lashes—a look that might have been coy but wasn't. "I wasn't sure if I should let on that he's a murder suspect, so I pretended I was doing follow-up for the research he participated in for our department. I told the professor I hadn't been able to get hold of him—which isn't a lie. He confirmed that Alex didn't return to classes this semester."

"We already knew that. Did you find out anything else?"

"I'm getting to that."

"Sorry. Go on."

She sat up straighter, prepared to give a report. He imagined her in the classroom, making a presentation. She was probably a good teacher—well-spoken and direct. Pleasant to listen to, which probably wasn't a requirement, but he was sure it helped. He liked listening to her, and he liked sitting across from her like this, breathing in the faint floral scent of her soap and enjoying the way the light of the lamp beside her illuminated her skin. "Alex is studying psychology," she said. "So I asked the professor what kind of person he thought Alex was. He said he was superficial."

Brodie considered the word. An unusual choice. "What do you think he meant?"

"He said Alex struck him as someone playing a part. He knew how to act like a serious student or a popular friend, but the professor always had the sense that beneath the surface, there wasn't much there. Or maybe, that there was something darker there that Alex didn't want to show to anyone else."

"Did you ask the professor if he thought Alex was a sociopath?"

"No. And I don't think he'd make that kind of diagnosis on the basis of their relationship. It wouldn't be professional."

"I'm no psychologist, but I'd say a man who kills eight women in cold blood doesn't have normal emotions or reactions."

"I wouldn't disagree." She met his gaze and he felt the zing of attraction. However else they had both changed in the past five years, they hadn't lost this sense of physical connection. He had always believed the physical side of a relationship was the most superficial, based on hormones and basic drives. With Emily, even this felt different.

"Did the professor say anything else?" he asked, determined to keep things loose and professional. He had meant what he said to Travis about coming here to do a job, not to resume a relationship with Emily. After all, she had made it clear when she had refused his proposal that she didn't see him as the kind of man she wanted to spend her life with.

"Only that Alex was very intelligent, made good grades when he applied himself and had expressed an interest in going into law enforcement work," she said. "Specifically, he mentioned he wanted to be a criminal profiler."

Another surprise. "That's interesting. And a little unnerving. I hate to think law enforcement would be attractive to someone like that."

"I don't know—if you wanted to commit crimes, doing it as a cop, where you would be privy to all the information about the investigation, would allow you to stay one step ahead of the people looking for you. You might even be able to guide them to look in the wrong direction."

"Now I'm a little unnerved that you've put so much thought into this." He tried for a teasing tone, letting her know he wasn't serious.

"You asked me to get inside Alex's head." She shifted position on the sofa. "Though I have to admit, it's not the most comfortable place to be."

"Do you have any ideas where he might be hiding out, or what his next move might be?" Brodie asked.

"I'm a researcher, not a clairvoyant," she said. "But I am working on it. The case feels really personal now, with Denise's death. I mean, I knew a lot of the women he's killed, but this hits a little close to home."

He nodded, but said nothing, debating whether he should mention his concerns about a connection to her.

She must have sensed his hesitation. She leaned toward him, her gaze searching. "What aren't you telling me?" she asked.

"I don't want to alarm you."

"I'm already alarmed."

He blew out a breath. Maybe if he shared his theories, she'd help blow them out of the water. "I'm wondering if you might be on Alex's radar as a possible target," he said. "If, in fact, you're what brought him to Eagle Mountain to begin with."

"Why would you think that?"

"Maybe he fixated on you."

"He's killed eight other women and hasn't even threatened me."

"Maybe he's biding his time, waiting for the right opportunity."

She didn't look frightened—only skeptical. "And the other women were what—practice?"

"The first one might have been. Then he discovered he liked killing. Or maybe he's done this before, someplace else."

"I'm sure Travis has already thought of that," she said. "I don't think he found any like crimes."

"You're right. And Alex is young. His first murder may very well have been Kelly Farrow."

"I think it's just a coincidence that he ended up here," she said. "He came here to ice climb with his friend, they got stranded by the snow and he killed Kelly—maybe he'd always had a sick fantasy about killing a woman and he thought doing so in this out-of-the-way place, with a small sheriff's department, would be easier."

Brodie nodded. "And once he started, he felt compelled to continue."

"From what I've read, that's how it works with many serial killers—they're fulfilling an elaborate, engrossing fantasy."

Brodie hoped she wasn't part of that fantasy, but decided not to share that with her. He didn't want to frighten her—only make her more aware of possible danger. "I told Travis I'd asked you to help with the case," he said.

"What did he say about that?"

"He reluctantly agreed to let you help, but I don't think he was too happy about getting his little sister involved." Or about any possible involvement between Brodie and Emily.

"He and Gage both tend to be overprotective. I've learned to humor them and do what I want, anyway."

"They have a right to be concerned. I hope you took what we said this afternoon—about not going anywhere alone—seriously."

"I did."

"It applies to all the women here at the ranch, and all the women you know."

"We do talk about this, you know? I don't know any woman who goes anywhere by herself without being alert to her surroundings."

"When you live in a peaceful place like Eagle Mountain, I can see how it would be easy to get complacent."

"But I don't live in Eagle Mountain," she said. "I live in Fort Collins. And I have two brothers who are cops. I know more than I want to about how dangerous it can be out there."

"Point taken," he said. And maybe it was time to shift the conversation to something more mundane and less stressful. "How do you like living in the big city? It's a lot different from life here on the ranch."

"I love it," she said. "I really enjoy my work, and I like all the opportunities and conveniences of a bigger city."

Footsteps approached and they both turned toward the door as Travis entered. He stopped short. "Brodie, what are you doing here?"

"I dropped off the files from Denise Switcher's car," Brodie said. "The ones she was bringing to Emily."

"I could have brought them," Travis said. He was

studying Brodie as if he was a perp he suspected of a crime.

"I'm sure Brodie didn't want to bother you with such a little errand," Emily said. She turned to Brodie. "Thanks again for bringing them to me."

"It's been a long day," Travis said. "I'm sure Brodie wants to get to his cabin."

Brodie resisted the urge to needle Travis by protesting that he wasn't tired in the least and had been enjoying his visit with Emily. But the sheriff looked in no mood for teasing. For whatever reason, Travis still harbored hard feelings about Brodie and Emily's breakup. At times, the sheriff seemed more upset with Brodie than Emily did. Brodie stood. "Travis is right," he said. "And I've kept you long enough."

"I enjoyed your visit," Emily said. Brodie wondered if she was saying so to goad her overprotective brother, but she sounded as if she meant it.

"Yeah, we'll have to do it again sometime." He didn't miss the dark look Travis sent him, but sauntered past the sheriff, head up. Brodie hadn't come here intending to renew his relationship with Emily. But if that did end up happening, maybe it wouldn't be such a bad thing.

As long as the sheriff didn't decide to run him out of town first.

Chapter Six

Reviewing the student surveys would have to wait until after Wednesday's barbecue and bonfire, the latest in a series of events at the ranch that Emily was hosting in an attempt to entertain friends and family trapped in town by the weather. Wednesday morning found Emily in the kitchen with Bette and Rainey, reviewing the menu for the evening. "Good plain food to help warm folks up in the cold," Rainey declared after describing the chili she would make and the kabobs Bette would assemble. "The kind of food I've been making all my life."

The ranch cook was an angular woman in her late forties or early fifties, who had reigned over the Walker kitchen for the past decade. Though she shooed Emily and her friends out of the kitchen whenever they invaded that sacred territory, she had also been known to spoil the youngest Walker sibling with homemade cookies and grilled pimento cheese sandwiches at every opportunity. Rainey's son's recent incarceration had subdued the cook a little, but she had also confided to Emily's mother that she felt less stressed, since at least now she knew her son was somewhere safe, and not causing trouble for anyone else.

"Everything will be delicious," Emily said, and handed the menu back to Bette. "And I definitely want to keep this simple. This close to the wedding, I don't want to burden either one of you."

"She's got this, and the wedding, taken care of," Rainey said.

"Rainey has been a big help with the reception preparations," Bette said, quick to praise the woman who, on her initial arrival at the ranch, had been her biggest foe.

Emily's cell phone rang. She fished it from the back pocket of her jeans and her heart sped up when she saw Professor Brandt's number. "I have to take this," she said, and hurried from the room.

Alone in the sunroom, she answered the call. "Hello, Professor."

"Hello, Emily. I asked around about Alex Woodruff and I found out a few things, though I don't know if they'll help you much."

Emily grabbed a notebook and pen from the table and sat on the sofa. "I'm all ears."

"This is an odd situation," he said. "And I'll admit, I'm curious now, too. Alex doesn't have any close friends that I could find, though he spent more time with Tim Dawson than anyone else. Do you know him?"

"Yes."

"Oddly enough, Tim failed to return to school also," the professor said. "I wasn't able to learn anything about him. When I contacted his family, they didn't want to talk to me about him. His father hung up on me."

Maybe the Dawsons didn't want to reveal that their son had been killed while committing a crime, or that he was a suspect in a series of murders. Emily was pretty sure Travis had talked to Tim's parents, but she had no idea what had come of that conversation. "What about Alex's family?" she asked.

"He's apparently estranged from them, though he has a trust fund that pays for his schooling and living expenses, and from what I gather, anything else he wants."

"Oh." That explained how he was able to spend a month in Eagle Mountain with no worries about money.

"I have a name for you, of a young woman he apparently dated for a while. Grace Anders. She's a student here. You understand I can't give you her contact information."

"I understand." If she couldn't figure out how to get hold of Grace on her own, Brodie or Travis could help her.

"When you return to school, you shouldn't have much trouble finding her here on campus, if you want to talk to her."

"Okay, thank you. Anything else?"

"No, that's all. But do me a favor and let me know what you find out. Like I said, I'm curious now."

"I'll do that." Though if things went well, Professor Brandt would be able to read about Alex and his arrest for murder in the Denver papers.

She hung up the phone and stared at the name she had written on her pad. Grace Anders. She could give the name to Travis and have him or Gage or one of his officers contact the young woman. They were trained to elicit information from witnesses. But would Grace really confide in them? Wouldn't she be more likely to open up to another woman at the university, someone close to her own age?

She picked up her phone again and punched in the number for the sheriff's department. Adelaide answered, all crisp professionalism. "The sheriff is out at the moment," she said, after Emily identified herself.

"It's really you I want to talk to," Emily said. "I'm doing a little job for Travis and I need help finding a phone number for a friend of Alex Woodruff. Grace Anders, in Fort Collins."

"Travis did mention something about you helping with the case," Adelaide said. "He wasn't too happy about the idea, if I recall."

"I'm staying safe, just making a few phone calls for him," she said. "Can you find Grace Anders's number for me?"

"Hold on a minute."

Emily doodled in her notebook while she waited

for Adelaide. She was coloring in circles around the word *trust fund* when the older woman came back on the line and rattled off a phone number. "Thanks, Adelaide," Emily said, and hung up before the office manager could question her further.

Before she could lose courage, Emily dialed the number Adelaide had given her. On the third ring a young woman answered. "If you're trying to sell something, I'm not interested," she said.

"I'm not selling anything, I promise," Emily said. "I'm calling about Alex Woodruff."

The silence on the other end of the line was so complete, Emily feared Grace had hung up. "What about him?" she asked after a minute.

"My name is Emily Walker. I'm a grad student at the university. Is this Grace Anders?"

"Why are you calling me? What has Alex done?"

Emily thought it was interesting that Grace assumed Alex had done something. Something wrong? "I understand you dated him at one time."

"Not for months. I haven't had anything to do with him for months and I'd just as soon keep it that way."

No love lost in her tone, Emily decided. "I'm trying to help a friend who had a rather unpleasant encounter with Alex," she said. That wasn't a complete lie—Denise was her friend, and Alex had killed her. Emily was trying to help find him and see that he was punished for the crime.

"Sorry about your friend," Grace said. "Alex is a creep."

"But you went out with him."

"Because I didn't know he was a creep at first," Grace said. "He was good-looking and he could be charming. We had a good time, at first."

"But something happened to change that?" Emily prompted.

"What did he do to your friend? I mean, did he steal money from her or something?"

"Did he steal money from you?"

"No. He had plenty of money of his own. I just wondered."

"He didn't steal from my friend." How much should Emily say? She wanted Grace to feel comfortable confiding in her, but she couldn't say anything that might jeopardize Travis's case against Alex.

"Did he assault her?" Grace blurted. "I mean, rape her or something?"

"Or something."

Grace swore. "I knew it. I should have said something before, but what would I have said?"

"Did Alex rape you?" Emily asked, as gently as possible.

"No! Nothing like that. It was just… I got really bad vibes from him."

"What kind of vibes?" Emily asked. "I know that's a really personal question, but it could really help."

Grace sighed dramatically. "We had sex a couple of times and it was fine, and then he wanted to do things different." She paused, then continued, "It feels so icky even talking about it, but he wanted to choke me."

Emily gasped. "Choke you?"

"Yeah, you know that autoerotic thing some people do where they choke themselves while they're getting off. It's supposed to give you some super orgasm or something, but it's crazy. People have died like that."

"But he didn't want to choke himself—he wanted to choke you."

"You get how creepy that is, right? I told him no way. I was really freaked out."

"How did he react when you refused him?"

"He got all huffy. He really pressured me, and that made me freak out even more."

"Because you had a really bad vibe."

"Yeah. I guess. It just seemed to me that it wasn't the sex he was so into, but the choking. I was worried he might like it so much he wouldn't stop. Is that what happened to your friend?"

"Something like that. You've been really helpful. If the police were to contact you about this, would you be willing to talk to them?"

"I guess. I'm sorry about your friend."

"Do you know of any other women he dated?" she asked.

"No. Like I said, I've stayed as far away from him as I could. Somebody told me he didn't come back to school this semester. I was relieved to hear it."

"Did Alex ever threaten you?" Emily asked.

"No. I just never felt comfortable around him after the choking thing came up."

"You were smart to turn him down. You have good instincts."

"Maybe I've had too much practice dating creeps. I just want to meet a good guy, you know?"

They said goodbye and Emily reviewed the conversation, organizing her thoughts to present to Travis. Maybe Alex had merely been interested in experimenting sexually, but her instincts told her Grace had read him correctly—he wasn't so much interested in the sexual experience as he was in choking a woman and knowing what that felt like.

He hadn't choked his victims, but maybe he had ruled out that method after being turned down by Grace. Or maybe he had intended her to be his first victim. He could murder her, and if anyone found out, he could claim she had died accidentally while they were experimenting. He might even have been able to get away with it.

Maybe he *had* gotten away with it. Maybe somewhere in Denver was a young woman who had died at Alex's hands, though he hadn't yet been charged with the crime.

With trembling hands, Emily punched in Travis's number. "Are you calling to tell me you've decided to cancel the bonfire tonight?" he asked.

"No! Why would I do that?"

"I told Lacy I thought you should. I'm concerned

Alex will try to repeat his performance at the scavenger hunt."

"Alex is not invited to this party."

"That might not stop him."

"It's too late to cancel the bonfire," she said, trying to quell her annoyance and not succeeding. "All the invitations have already gone out, and the ranch hands have been accumulating a mountain of scrap wood and brush that needs to be burned. Not to mention Rainey and Bette have been cooking party food for days. I'm certainly not going to tell them their extra work will be wasted."

"Which is pretty much what Lacy said. But she agreed that I could station a deputy and one of the ranch hands at the gate to check the ID of every person who enters against your guest list. So I'll need a copy of the list, first chance you get."

"All right." Part of her thought this was overkill, but the rest of her was grateful for this extra measure of safety.

"If you didn't call about the party, why did you call?" Travis asked.

"I talked to a woman Alex used to date," she said. "She said they broke up when he tried to talk her into letting him strangle her while they had sex."

"That's interesting. Does she have any idea where he is right now?"

"No. She hasn't had anything to do with him for a couple of months. But do you think this is how he started? What if some other woman agreed to his proposal and she died and everyone thought it was an accident, when really it was murder?"

"I haven't found anything like that in my research, but I can add it to his file."

"You could call someone in Fort Collins and Denver and try to find out."

"I could. But that won't help us discover where Alex is right now, and that's what I need to know if I'm going to stop him."

"No one in Fort Collins knows where he is," she said. "His professor told me he didn't have any friends but Tim, and he's estranged from his parents. Oh, and he has a big trust fund that pays for everything."

"Yes, we knew that."

"Then why did you even ask me to try to find out about him?"

"You've learned useful information," Travis said. "I don't want you to think I don't appreciate your help. But we really need to focus on where Alex might be hiding right now. Did he know anyone in Eagle Mountain before he arrived here? Does he have any relatives who live here? Did he ever complete an outdoor survival course or express an interest in winter camping?"

If Travis wanted her to ask questions like that, why hadn't he given her a list? "I don't think any of the people I talked to know those things," she said.

"Maybe no one does," Travis said. "But it's important to try everything we can think of. Is there anything else you need to tell me?"

"No."

"Then I have to go."

He ended the call and Emily frowned at her phone, fighting frustration. She felt like she had learned something important about Alex, but Travis was right—it wasn't going to help them find him and stop him. The longer it took to locate him, the more time he had to attack and kill another woman.

She studied her notebook, hoping for inspiration that didn't come. "Emily?"

She turned toward the door, where Lacy stood. "The ranch hands brought up that load of hay bales you asked for," she said. "They want to know what to do with them."

"Sure thing." She jumped up, pushing aside thoughts of Alex for now. Time to distract everyone else—and herself—from the danger lurking just outside their doors.

For the rest of the day, Emily focused on making sure the party was a success, and counted it a good sign that, though the highway was still closed due to multiple avalanches, no new snow had fallen in a couple of days, and clouds had receded to reveal a star-spangled night sky and an almost-full moon like a shining silver button overhead.

As an added bonus, though the wedding favors and guest book hadn't been delivered before the road closed again, Paige Riddell and her significant other, DEA agent Rob Allerton, had arrived and moved into the last empty guest cabin. Lacy was thrilled her friend had made it and had thanked Emily half a dozen times today for arranging the bonfire.

All the guests seemed happy to be here, gathering in a semicircle as Travis, Gage and Emily's father lit the bonfire, then cheering as it caught and blazed to life. Even before the blaze gave off much warmth, the sight of it made everyone more animated. The flames popped and crackled as they climbed the tower of old pallets, scrap wood and brush the ranch hands had spent days assembling; the sparks rose like glitter floating up into the black sky, the scent of wood smoke mingling with the aroma of barbecue and mulled cider.

From the fire, guests gravitated to a buffet set up under tents. Rainey and Bette had prepared big vats of chili, pans of corn bread and half a dozen different salads. They had also arranged skewers of kabobs and sausages guests could toast over the fire. Guests could opt for cookies for dessert, or create their own s'mores.

Seating was provided by hay bales draped in blankets and buffalo robes, shaped into surprisingly comfortable couches—some long enough for half a dozen people, others just the right size for cuddling for two. Two of the ranch hands played guitar and sang for the appreciative crowd. Alcoholic and nonalcoholic beverages added to the festivities.

"Travis tells me you're the genius behind all this." Brodie's voice, low and velvety, pulled Emily's attention from the music. She hoped the dim lighting hid the warm flush that seemed to engulf her body at his approach. He indicated the crowd around the bonfire. "It's a great party."

"Travis wanted to cancel the whole thing, but I had Lacy in my corner," she said.

"He doesn't look too upset right now." Brodie nodded toward the sheriff, who was slow dancing with Lacy on the edge of the firelight, her head on his shoulder, both dancers' eyes half-closed.

Emily couldn't help but smile at the lovebirds. "They're so good together," she said. "It's great to see Travis so happy."

"Gage has found his match, too," Brodie said.

Emily shifted her attention from Travis to her other brother, who sat on a hay bale with his wife, Maya. The two were feeding each other toasted marshmallows and laughing, eyes shining as they gazed at one another. Emily sighed. "I never would have guessed my two brothers could be such romantics," she said.

"Are you kidding? When it comes to love, most men are completely at a woman's mercy. We may not always show our romantic side, but it's definitely there."

"I'm not talking about buying a woman flowers and delivering a convincing line to get her to go out with you—or to go to bed with you," Emily said.

"Neither am I. I think most people want to be in relationships, to love and be loved. Maybe one of the reasons a lot of men—and maybe women, too—have a hard time expressing that desire is that they know it's so important. They're really afraid of messing things up and getting it wrong."

Brodie was the last person in the world she had ever expected she'd have a philosophical conversation about love with. "Excuse me?" she asked. "Are you sure you're really Brodie Langtry? Mr. Heartbreaker?" He certainly hadn't hinted that he was so keen on that kind of deep relationship when the two of them had been together. And she still wasn't sure she believed he had never received the letter she had sent to him after their breakup. Pretending he'd never seen it made him look much better than if he had read the letter and decided to blow her off—which was what she had always believed.

"I grew up," he said, her own image shining back at her in the reflection of the firelight in his eyes. "We all do. Besides, I was never as shallow as you thought I was. When someone is important to me, I will do anything to protect them and support them."

Now he was getting really hard for her to believe. "Have you ever had a serious relationship with a woman in your life?" she asked.

"Once."

A sharp pain pinched her chest. Who was this woman who had captured his heart? And why did it hurt to hear about her? Emily wet her lips. "When was that?"

"A long time ago."

She thought she heard real regret in his voice, but why was she feeling sorry for him? "I don't believe you," she said. "You can have any woman you want. If you commit to one, you have to give up all the others, so why should you?"

"What about you?" he asked. "Are you serious about someone? Or have you ever been?"

He was the only man she'd made the mistake of falling for. "I'm getting my degree and focusing on my career. I don't have time for a relationship."

He moved closer, blocking the firelight, the sheepskin collar of his heavy leather coat brushing against the nylon of her down-filled parka. Layers of fabric separated them, yet she felt the contact, like current flowing through an electrical cord once it was plugged in. She couldn't make out his features in the darkness, but was sure he was watching her. "Now who's avoiding commitment?" he asked.

She told herself she should move away, but couldn't make her feet obey the command. "I'm not avoiding anything," she said.

"Except me. You don't have to run from me, Emily. I would never hurt you."

Hurt wasn't always a matter of intent—maturity had taught her that, at least. This knowledge made it easier for her to forgive him, but she wasn't going to forget anytime soon how easily he had wounded her. She would have told anyone that she had gotten over him long ago, then he showed up here at the ranch and all the old feelings came surging back like the tide rushing in. No good would come of revisiting all that.

"I have to go check on the food," she said, finally forcing herself to take a step back, and then another.

He didn't come after her, just stood and watched her run away. Maybe he didn't pursue her because he didn't really want her, she told herself as she hurried toward the buffet table.

Or maybe he didn't chase her because he was so sure that if he bided his time, he could have her, anyway. That, on some level, she had never really stopped being his.

BRODIE LET EMILY walk away. Maybe what they both needed right now was space. He had never expected to be so drawn to her. He had thought he was over her years ago. He'd been angry and hurt when she turned down his marriage proposal, and had spent more than a few months nursing his hurt feelings and wounded pride.

And now that he was back in town, Emily's family acted as if he was the villain in the whole bad scene. Had Emily made up some story about him dumping her, instead of admitting that she'd turned him down? She didn't strike him as the type to lie about something like that, but as he had told her, they had both done a lot of growing up in the past five years.

He helped himself to a kabob from the buffet table and tried his hand grilling it over the fire. Gage, a skewered sausage in hand, joined him. Of the two brothers, Gage had been the friendliest since Brodie's return to Eagle Mountain. "How's it going?" Gage asked.

"Okay." Brodie glanced around to make sure no one could overhear. "I'm trying to figure out why your family is giving me the cold shoulder. I mean, they're all polite, but not exactly welcoming."

Gage slanted a look at him. "You dated Emily for a while, right?"

"Yes. Five years ago. And then we broke up. It happens. That doesn't make me the bad guy."

Gage rotated the sausage and moved it closer to the flames. "I was away at school when that all went down, so I don't know much about it," he said. "I do know when I asked about it when I came home for the holidays, everybody clammed up about it. I got the impression you dumped Emily and broke her heart. You were one of Travis's best friends, so I guess he saw it as some kind of betrayal."

"I asked your sister to marry me and she turned me down," Brodie said. "That's not exactly dumping her."

"Does Travis know that?"

"I'm sure he does. Emily didn't have any reason to lie about it."

Gage shook his head. "Then maybe you'd better

ask Travis what's on his mind. You know him—he keeps his feelings to himself, most of the time."

"Maybe I will." But not tonight. Brodie looked across the fire to where Travis sat with Lacy in the golden glow of the fire, their heads together, whispering. The sheriff looked happier and more relaxed than he had since Brodie had arrived. Amazing what love could do for a person.

Someone shouting made him tense, and he turned to see Dwight helping Rob Allerton into the circle of firelight. Rob dropped onto a hay bale and pushed Dwight away, as Paige rushed to him. "What happened?" she asked, gingerly touching a darkening bruise on his forehead.

"I left my phone back in our cabin and decided to go get it so I could show someone some pictures I have on it," Rob said. "As I neared the ranch house, I noticed someone moving around by the cars. At first I thought it was someone leaving the party early, but as I drew nearer, the guy bolted and ran straight at me. He had a tire iron or a club or something like that in his hand." Rob touched the bruise and winced. "I guess I'm lucky he only struck me a glancing blow, but I fell, and by the time I got to my feet and went looking for him, he had vanished." He looked up and found Travis in the crowd gathered around him. "I think he did something to your sheriff's department SUV."

Brodie followed Travis, Gage and most of the rest of the guests over to the parking area in front of the house. Travis's SUV was parked in the shadows at the far end of a line of cars and trucks. The sheriff played the beam of a flashlight over the vehicle, coming to rest on the driver's-side door. Someone had spray-painted a message in foot-high, bright red letters: *ICE COLD*.

Chapter Seven

Emily dragged herself into the sheriff's department the next morning, the two cups of coffee she had forced down with breakfast having done little to put her in a better mood. She hadn't slept much after the party broke up last night—something she probably shared in common with everyone else in attendance at this meeting the sheriff had called. Most of the law enforcement personnel who gathered in the conference room had searched the ranch and surrounding area for Alex Woodruff late into the previous night. Once again, after leaving his blood-red taunt on Travis's SUV, he had disappeared into the darkness.

She took her place to Travis's left at the conference table, nodding in greeting at the others around the table and avoiding lingering too long when her gaze fell on Brodie. She had missed him at breakfast this morning. Her mother had mentioned that he'd left early with Travis. Though the two men hadn't been friendly since Brodie's arrival at the ranch, they did seem to work together well.

Her feelings for Brodie seemed to fluctuate between regret and relief. Regret that they couldn't pick up the easy exchange they had enjoyed Tuesday evening in the sunroom. Relief that she didn't have to revisit the tension between them beside the bonfire last night. Other people got through situations like this and were able to put the past behind them. She and Brodie would learn to do that, too.

Travis stood and everyone fell silent. "I think you all know my sister, Emily," he said. "She is acquainted with Alex Woodruff and is completing her master's degree in behavioral economics. I've asked her to sit in on some meetings, to help us try to get into Alex's mind in hopes of anticipating his next move."

"I pity you, being in that guy's mind," someone— she thought it might be Ryder Stewart—said from the other end of the table.

Travis ignored the comment and projected a map of Rayford County onto a wall screen. "As I believe all of you know, someone—we're operating on the assumption that it was Alex—vandalized my department SUV last night at my family's ranch during a party."

"How did he get by the security you had set up?" wildlife officer Nate Harris asked.

"He parked around a curve, out of sight of the guards," Travis said. "He approached the ranch house on foot, and circled around through the trees. We were able to trace his movements that far at first light."

"He must have run track." Rob Allerton had joined them this morning, the bruise on his forehead an angry purple, matching the half-moons under his eyes. "He raced out of there like a gazelle."

Travis projected a color photo of his SUV onto the wall screen. The large red letters stood out against the Rayford County Sheriff's logo. "He's always enjoyed taunting us. This seems to represent an acceleration of that."

"He knows we know who he is and he doesn't care," Ryder Stewart declared.

"He thinks he's better than all of us," Brodie said.

"We're looking for anywhere Alex might be hiding," Travis said. "We've ruled out the two sets of forest service summer cabins where we know he and Tim Dawson spent time before." He circled these sites in red on the image. "We know Alex and Tim used an unoccupied vacation home as a hideout previously, so we're working our way through unoccupied homes but we haven't hit anything there, either. We've also published Alex's picture in the paper, on posters around town and on all the social media outlets. We've alerted people to let us know if they spot him."

"If he's using someone's vacation home, the neighbors are bound to see him," Dwight said.

"Maybe he's using a disguise," Deputy Jamie Douglas said.

"Alex was in the drama club at the university," Emily said. "But I don't think he would hide in a place with a lot of people—not now when he knows you've identified him. He takes risks, but they're calculated risks." She had lain awake for a long time last night thinking about this, and searched for the right words to share her conclusions. "He knows you're looking for him, and he wants to be free to come and go as he pleases. That freedom is important to him—he has to be in charge, not allowing you to dictate his movements. Showing up at the ranch last night and vandalizing your vehicle is another way of asserting that freedom."

"He could have moved into an abandoned mine," Nate said from his seat beside Jamie. "There are plenty of those around."

Travis nodded. "We'll check those out."

"He could be in a cave," Dwight said.

"He could be," Travis said. "But remember—wherever he is has to be accessible by a road."

Emily leaned forward, trying to get a better look at the map. "What's that symbol on the map, near Dixon Pass?" she asked.

Travis studied the image, then rested the pointer on a stick figure facing downhill. "Do you mean this? I think it's the symbol for an old ski area."

"Dixon Downhill," Gage said. "I think it's been closed since the eighties. When they widened the highway in the nineties, they covered over the old access road into the place."

"I think part of the old ski lift is still there,"

Dwight said. "But I'm pretty sure they bulldozed all the buildings."

"Gage, you and Dwight check it out," Travis said. "See if there are any habitable buildings there where Alex might be holed up."

"I'd like to go with them," Brodie said.

"All right," Travis agreed. "Dwight, you and Nate can work on the mines." He gave out assignments to the others on the team.

"What would you like me to do?" Emily asked, as the others gathered up their paperwork and prepared to depart.

"You can go home and write up your thoughts on Alex," Travis said.

A report he would dutifully read, file away and consider his obligation to her met. Her brother might have agreed to let Brodie ask for her help, but that didn't mean he was going to let her get very involved. "I'd like to talk to Jamie," she said. "She spent time with Alex's partner, Tim, when the two kidnapped her and her sister."

"Her statement is in the file I gave you," Travis said.

"I want to talk to her," she said, with more force behind the words.

Travis gave her a hard look, but she looked him in the eye and didn't back down. "All right," he said. "Set it up with her."

"I'll see if she can meet me for lunch." She started to leave, but he stopped her.

"Emily?"

She turned toward him again. "Yes?"

"Alex Woodruff is very dangerous. Don't get any ideas about trying to get close to him on your own."

A shudder went through her. "Why would I want to get close to a man who's murdered eight women? Travis, do you really think I'm that stupid?"

"You're not stupid," he said. "But you tend to always think the best of people."

She wondered if he was talking about more than Alex now. Was he also warning her away from Brodie?

"I'll be careful," she said. "And I won't do anything foolish." Not when it came to either man.

To REACH WHAT was left of the Dixon Downhill ski area, Brodie and Gage had to park at the barricades closing off the highway, strap on snowshoes and walk up the snow-covered pavement to a break in a concrete berm on the side of the road, where an old emergency access road lay buried under snow. Reflectors on trees defined the route. The two men followed the reflectors to a bench that was the remains of the road that had once led to the resort.

The resort itself had been situated in a valley below the pass, with lift-accessed skiing on both sides. "You can still see the cuts for the old ski runs from here." Gage pointed out the wide path cut through stands of tall spruce and fir.

"Is that the lift line there?" Brodie indicated a

cable running through the trees to their right. A couple of rusting metal chairs dangled crookedly from the braided line.

"I think so. There's the lift shack, at the top."

The small building that housed the engine that ran the old rope-tow lift really was a shack, cobbled together from rough lumber and tin, a rusting pipe jutting from the roof that was probably the engine exhaust. Brodie took out a pair of binoculars and glassed the area. From this angle, at least, it didn't look as if anyone had been down there in a long time.

"They used old car motors to power some of these things," Gage said. "I'd like to get a look at this one."

"Does the lift still run?" Brodie asked.

"I don't think so," Gage said. "Though if a mechanic messed with it, he might be able to get it going again. Those old motors weren't that sophisticated, and it's been out of the weather."

Gage led the way as they descended into the valley. With no traffic on the closed highway above, and thick snow muffling their steps, the only sounds were the occasional click of the ski poles they were using against a chunk of ice, and their labored breathing on the ascent.

Brodie tried not to think of the mountain of snow on either side of them. "Did you check with the avalanche center before we came down here?" he asked.

"No," Gage said. "We probably should have, but I was too eager to get down here and see what we could see." He stopped and glanced up toward the highway. "We'll be all right as long as he doesn't try to climb up and disturb the snowpack up there."

Brodie hoped Gage was right. After ten minutes of walking, they were forced to stop, the old road completely blocked by a snowslide, the wall of snow rising ten feet over their heads. "I think it's safe to say no one has been down here in a while," Gage said. "This didn't just happen." Dirt and debris dusted the top of the slide, and the ends of tree branches jutting out of the snow were dry and brown.

"At least now we know no one has been here," Gage said.

"Is this road the only way in?" Brodie asked.

"In summer, it might be possible to climb down the rock face from the highway," Gage said. "Though I wouldn't want to try it." He shook his head. "Even if Alex could get here, there's no place for him to stay. That lift shack isn't going to offer much shelter. At this elevation nighttime temperatures would be brutal. And the only way in and out is to go up this road—which is blocked—or scramble straight up."

"Wherever he is, it's somewhere he can go with ease," Brodie said. "This isn't it."

Gage clapped him on the back. "Come on. Let's go back."

The trip up was slower going, in deep snow up a steep grade. "We should have thought to bring a snowmobile," Gage said when they paused halfway up to rest.

Brodie took a bottle of water from his pack and

drank deeply. "And then if Alex had been down there, he would have heard us coming miles away."

"He's not down there." Gage looked around at the world of white. "I wish I knew where he is."

Brodie started to replace the water bottle in his pack when a loud report made him freeze. "What was that?" he asked.

"It sounded like a gunshot." Gage put a hand on his weapon.

"Not close," Brodie said. "Maybe someone target shooting?"

"It sounded like it's up on the highway," Gage said. "Maybe a blowout on one of the road machines?"

"Let's get out of here," Brodie said. They started walking again, but had gone only a few steps when an ominous rumble sent his heart into his throat. He took off running, even as a wave of snow and debris flowed down the slope toward them.

Chapter Eight

Emily arranged to meet Deputy Jamie Douglas for lunch at a new taco place on the south end of town. The former gas station had half a dozen tables inside, and a busy drive-up window. Jamie, her dark hair in a neat twist at the nape of her neck, waved to Emily from one of the tables. "Thanks for agreeing to talk to me," Emily said, joining the deputy at the table.

"Sure. What can I do for you?"

"Let's order lunch and I'll fill you in."

They ordered at a window at the back of the room, then collected their food and returned to the table. "Travis asked me to put together a kind of profile of Alex Woodruff," Emily said when they were situated. "Not as an official profiler, but because I knew him slightly from the university and he hoped I'd have some insights. You probably spent more time with his partner, Tim, than anyone else, so I thought you might have some thoughts I could add to my assessment."

Jamie spooned salsa over her tacos. "I never even met Alex," she said.

"I know. But I think more information about Tim would help me clarify some things about their relationship."

"Sure. I'll try. What do you need to know?"

"I read your report, so I know the facts about what happened when Tim and Alex kidnapped you, but I'm more interested in other behavioral things."

"Like what?"

"When you came to, you and your sister were alone in the cabin with Tim?"

"Yes."

"And he told you he was waiting for Alex to return?"

"That's right. Well, he never named him, but we knew his partner was Alex."

"Did you get the impression that Alex was the leader—that Tim was looking to him to make the decisions?"

"Yes. Tim got a phone call from his partner— from Alex—who apparently told him he had to kill us by himself. Tim didn't like this, so then they agreed that Tim would bring us to wherever Alex was waiting, and they would kill us together."

"Do you think the idea of the killings started with Alex, or was it Tim's idea?"

"Definitely Alex. Tim said the first killing freaked him out, but then he started to like it. Or, at least, he liked getting away with the crimes."

"Alex must have recognized a similar personality to his own," Emily said.

Jamie nodded. "I guess it's like they say—birds of a feather flock together."

"My understanding is that Tim acted as the decoy, dressed as a woman, while Alex came up out of the woods and attacked women?" Emily asked.

"Yes. And Tammy Patterson's description of her ordeal confirms that." Tammy was a reporter for the *Eagle Mountain Examiner* who had managed to get away from Alex and Tim after they waylaid her one snowy afternoon.

"I don't think the two were equal partners," Emily said. "Alex was dominant. He's the man who chose the targets, and probably the one who did the actual killing. Tim was his helper. I wonder if Tim would have eventually killed on his own, without Alex around to goad him into doing it."

"I don't know," Jamie said. "But I believe Tim was prepared to kill me and Donna on his own. At least, that's what he told Alex."

"How is your sister doing after this ordeal?" Emily asked. Donna was a pleasant young woman with developmental disabilities who worked at Eagle Mountain Grocery.

"She's doing good." Jamie's smile at the mention of her sister was gentle. "She had some nightmares, but Nate has moved in with us and that's helped. She gets along really great with him, and she says having him in the house at night makes her feel safer." She blushed. "He makes me feel safer, too."

Emily hadn't missed that Jamie had been sitting next to Nate Harris at the meeting this morning. "It's great that the two of you got together," she said.

Jamie rotated the small diamond solitaire on the third finger of her left hand. "We're going to be married in the spring and Donna is almost more excited than I am."

"Congratulations." Emily couldn't quite hide her surprise. The last she had heard, Jamie and Nate had only recently started dating. "You obviously don't believe in long engagements."

"We were high school sweethearts, you know," Jamie said. "We broke up when he went away to college. I thought it was because he was eager to be free of me and date other people. He thought he was doing me a favor, not leaving me tied down to a man who wasn't around. Anyway, I guess we needed that time apart to really appreciate each other."

Emily nodded. So Jamie and Nate weren't strangers who just got together. They had dated and split up before—like her and Brodie. Except the situation with Brodie was entirely different. The circumstances of their split, and everything that had happened afterward, made things so much more awkward between them now.

Jamie's radio crackled with words that were, to Emily, unintelligible, but Jamie set down the glass of tea she had been sipping and jumped to her feet, her face pale. "I have to go," she said.

"What is it?" Emily asked, as the alarm from the fire station down the street filled the air. "What's happened?"

"An avalanche on Dixon Pass," Jamie said, already moving toward the door. "Gage and Brodie may be caught in it!"

As THE WAVE of white moved down the hill toward him, Brodie tried to think what he was supposed to do. He had taken a backcountry rescue course once, and he struggled to recall what the instructor had said.

Then the avalanche of snow was on him, hitting him with the force of a truck, sending him sprawling, struggling for breath. Instinct took over and he began swimming in the snow, fighting to reach the surface before it hardened around him like concrete. He fought hard for each stroke, his thoughts a jumble of images—of Gage's startled face just before the snow hit, of his mother the last time he had seen her and finally of Emily.

Emily, the hardness gone out of her eyes when she looked at him, head tilted to look up at him, lips slightly parted in a silent invitation for a kiss...

Then he popped to the surface of the snowslide, like a surfer thrust forward by the momentum of a wave, gasping in the achingly cold air. A tree branch glanced off his shoulder with a painful blow, then a rock bounced off his head, making him cry out.

Wrenching his head around, he saw that he was on the very edge of the slide, which had probably saved him. He struggled his way out of the snow's grip, like a man floundering out of quicksand. "Gage!" he screamed, then louder, "Gage!"

Relief surged through him as a faint cry greeted him. He fought his way toward it, clawing at the snow with numbed and aching hands, repeatedly calling, then waiting for the response to guide him in the right direction. "Gage! Gage!"

At last he located the source of the cries, and dug into the snow, first with his hands, then with a tree branch. He uncovered Gage's leg, the familiar khaki uniform twisted around his calf, then he dug his way up to Gage's head. When he had cleared away enough snow, he helped Gage sit up. They slumped together in the snow, gasping for air. A thin line of blood trickled from a cut on Gage's forehead, eventually clotting in the cold.

"We need to get out of here," Gage said after many minutes.

"We need help," Brodie countered, and shifted to reach his cell phone. The signal wasn't good, but it might be enough. He dialed 911 and said the words most likely to rush help their way without long explanations. "Officer needs assistance, top of Dixon Pass."

The phone slipped from his numb grasp and he

watched with an air of detachment as it skidded down the slope. Gage struggled to extract his own phone, then stared at the shattered screen. "They'll find us," he said, and lay back on the snow and closed his eyes.

Brodie wanted to join his friend in lying down for a nap. Fatigue dragged at him like a concrete blanket. He couldn't remember when he'd been so exhausted. But the danger of freezing out here in the snow was real. "Wake up, Gage," he said, trying to put some force behind the words. "You don't want to survive an avalanche only to die of hypothermia."

"There are worse ways to go," Gage said. But he sat up and looked up the slope, to the scarred area that showed the path of the avalanche.

"What do you think set it off?" Brodie asked.

"I don't know. Maybe that sound we heard earlier. That engine backfiring."

"Or the gunshot." The more Brodie thought about that report, the more it sounded to him like a gunshot.

"Somebody target shooting in the national forest?" Gage suggested. "Sound carries funny in the canyons."

"Maybe," Brodie said. "But what if someone set off the snowslide deliberately?"

"Why would they do that?"

"Because they didn't like us taking a look at the old ski resort?"

"I don't know who would object. And you saw

yourself—no one has been down there in weeks. Since before that older snowslide."

"Can we find out when that snowslide happened?" Brodie asked.

"Probably," Gage said. "Maybe. I don't really know." He tilted his head. "Does that sound like a siren to you?"

It did, and half an hour later a search-and-rescue team had descended and was helping them back up the slope. The SAR director had wanted to strap Brodie and Gage into Stokes baskets and winch them up the slope, but the two victims had persuaded him they were capable of standing and walking out under their own power, with only a little help from the SAR volunteers.

An hour after that, Brodie was in his guest cabin on the Walker ranch, fortified with a sandwich and coffee, fresh from a hot shower and contemplating a nap.

A knock on the door interrupted those plans, however. He glanced through the peephole, then jerked open the door. "Emily, what are you doing here?" he asked.

She moved past him into the room, her face pale against her dark hair. "I wanted to make sure you were all right," she said.

"I'm fine." He rolled his shoulders, testing the statement. "A little bruised and tired, but okay."

She touched his arm, and the purpling bruise where he had collided with a tree branch or boulder in his frantic effort to escape the snowslide. That light, silken touch against his bare skin sent a current of heat through him.

He moved toward her, drawn by the scent of her mingling in the lingering steam from his shower. Her eyes widened, as if she was only just now seeing him—all of him, naked except for a pair of jeans, his skin still damp, droplets lingering in the hair on his chest.

She jerked her gaze back to his bruised arm. "You should put something on this," she said, her voice husky.

"Would you do it for me?"

"All right."

He retreated to the bathroom and fetched the ointment from his first-aid kit. Did he imagine her hand trembled when he handed it to her? Her touch was steady enough as she smoothed the ointment on, so careful and caring, and so incredibly sensuous, as if she was caressing not only his wound, but the invisible hurts inside of him.

She capped the tube of ointment and raised her eyes to meet his. Time stopped in that moment, and he had the sensation of being in a dream as he slid his arm around her waist and she leaned into him, reaching up to rest her fingers against the side of his neck, rising on her toes to press her lips to his.

He had a memory of kissing her when she had been a girl, but she kissed like a woman now, sure and wanting, telling him what she desired without the need for words. When she pressed her body to his, he pulled her more tightly against him, and when she parted her lips, he met the thrust of her tongue with his own. He willingly drowned in that kiss, losing himself until he had to break free, gasping, his heart pounding.

She opened her eyes and stared up at him with a dreamy, dazed expression. Then her vision cleared, eyes opening wider. She let out a gasp and pulled away. "I can't do this," she said, and fled, out of his arms and out the door before he had time to react.

He wanted to go after her but didn't. He lay back on the bed and stared up at the ceiling, marveling at the twisted turn his life had taken, bringing him back here, to this woman, after so long.

And wondering where it all might lead.

Chapter Nine

Emily read through the first of the surveys her professor had sent for her to review—then read through it again, nothing having registered on the first pass. Her head was too full of Brodie—of the pressure of his lips on hers, the strength of his arms around her, the taste of his kisses. For all she had been enthralled by him five years ago, she had never felt such passion back then. The Brodie she had faced in his cabin yesterday had been more serious, with a depth she hadn't recognized before. He was stronger—and far more dangerous to her peace.

At this point in her life, she thought she could have handled a merely physical fling with a fun, hot guy. But she could never think of Brodie as merely a fling. And she didn't know if she would ever be able to completely trust him with her feelings. Even five years before, as crazy as she was about him, she had never been able to fully believe that his feelings for her were more than superficial. She was another conquest, another victim of his charm. He hadn't acted particularly torn up when she had turned down his marriage proposal, and he hadn't made any effort to persuade her to change her mind.

Even if he hadn't received the letter she had sent to him later, if he had really loved her, wouldn't he have kept in touch? He could have used his friendship with Travis as an excuse to at least check on her. But he had simply vanished from her life. That knowledge didn't leave a good feeling behind, and it made getting involved with him again far too risky.

But she wasn't going to think about him now. She had work to do. Determined to focus, she started reading through the survey once more. She had just finished her read-through and was starting to make notes when her cell phone buzzed, startling her.

Half afraid it might be Brodie, she swiped open the screen, then sagged with relief when she read her brother's name. "Hi, Travis," she answered.

"There's someone here at the station I think you should talk to," he said.

"Who is it?"

"Ruth Schultz. She says she knows you."

Emily searched her memory for the name, but came up blank. "I don't think—"

"Hang on a minute… She says you knew her as Ruth Parmenter."

"Ruthie!" Emily smiled. They had been classmates in high school. "Why does she want to see me?"

"It has to do with the case. Could you come down and talk to her?"

Puzzled, but intrigued, Emily glanced at the folder full of surveys. Not exactly scintillating reading. And not all that pressing, either, not with a murderer on the loose. "Sure. Tell her I'll be there in half an hour."

Twenty-five minutes later, Adelaide looked up from her desk when Emily entered the sheriff's department. "Mrs. Schultz is in interview room one." Adelaide pointed down the hall. "She said she can stay until twelve thirty. That's when her youngest gets out of half-day kindergarten."

"All right." Emily headed past the desk, intending to stop by Travis's office first to ask what exactly she was supposed to be talking about with Ruthie, but before she could reach the sheriff's door, Brodie stepped out and intercepted her. "Travis had to leave, so he asked me to sit in with you and Mrs. Schultz," he said.

Running into him this way, when she hadn't had time to prepare, unsettled her. She took a deep, steadying breath, but that was a mistake, since all it did was fill her head with the masculine scent of him—leather and starch and the herbal soap that had surrounded them last night. She stared over his left shoulder and managed to keep her voice steady. "What is this all about?"

"She says her younger sister, Renee, is missing."

Emily had a vague memory of a girl who had been three years behind her in school—a pretty, sandy-haired flirt who had been popular with the older boys, and thus, unpopular with the older girls. "How long has she been missing?"

"Four days. At first Mrs. Schultz thought she had left town when the road opened and got caught when the road closed again. But she hasn't answered any calls or texts and that's not like her."

"Maybe her phone lost its charge or broke," Emily said. "Or maybe she's somewhere she doesn't want her sister to know about."

Brodie frowned. "Maybe. But Mrs. Schultz is worried because she said Renee knew Alex. She went out with him at least once."

Emily sucked in her breath. "That is a frightening thought. But why does she want to talk to me?"

"Because you knew Renee, and you know Alex. Travis explained you were helping us put together a profile of Alex and he thought the information she had might help. But most of all, I think she's looking for some reassurance from you that her sister is all right."

"I don't think I can give her that," Emily said.

"Probably not. But maybe telling her story to a friendly face—someone who isn't a cop—may help her."

"Then of course I'll talk to her."

Emily remembered Ruthie Parmenter as an elfin figure with a mop of curly brown hair and freckles, a star on the school track team, president of the debate club and senior class president. She had talked about going to college on the East Coast, then taking off for Europe with a camera, maybe becoming a war correspondent or a travel journalist or something equally exciting and adventurous.

The woman who looked up when Emily and Brodie entered the interview room was still lithe and freckle-faced, though her hair had been straightened and pulled back from her face by a silver clip. She wore a tailored blouse and jeans, and an anxious expression. "Emily, it's so good to see you," she said, standing and leaning over the table to give Emily a hug. "You still look just the same. I'd have recognized you anywhere."

Emily wasn't so sure she would have recognized Ruthie. Her former classmate looked older and more careworn, though maybe that was only from worrying about her sister. She indicated Brodie. "This is Agent Brodie Langtry, with the Colorado Bureau of Investigation."

"Yes, Brodie and I have met." The smile she gave him held an extra warmth, and Emily inwardly recoiled at a sudden pinch of jealousy. Seriously? Was she going to turn into that kind of cliché?

"Why don't we have a seat?" she said, pulling out a chair.

They sat, Brodie at the end of the table and the two women facing each other. "Brodie said you haven't been able to get in touch with your sister," Emily began.

"Yes. Not since Monday afternoon, when the road opened again for what was it—less than a day? I wasn't worried at first. I assumed she'd gone to Junction to shop and maybe take in a movie. But when I called the next day and she didn't answer, I was a little concerned. And when she didn't come to dinner last night, I knew something was wrong. It was my son's birthday—he just turned six. Renee would never have missed Ian's birthday."

"Was your sister dating anyone in particular?"

"No." She waved her hand, as if brushing aside the suggestion. "You know Renee—she always liked men, but she was never ready to settle down with anyone. She hasn't changed in that respect."

"But she had dated Alex Woodruff?" Emily asked.

"Yes." The faint lines on either side of her mouth deepened. "When I saw his picture in the paper and read that he was a person of interest in the Ice Cold Killer murders, my legs gave out and I had to sit down. And I knew I had to contact the sheriff. In case…" She paused and swallowed, then forced out the next words. "In case he's the reason Renee is missing."

Emily reached across and took Ruthie's hand and squeezed it. She could only imagine how worried Ruthie must be, but she wasn't going to offer hollow words of comfort. "When did Renee last go out with Alex?" she asked.

"I'm not positive, but I think they only had the one date. I think she would have told me if there was more than one—that was back on New Year's Eve.

She went with him to the Elks' New Year's dance. My husband and I met them there."

"Was that their first date?" Emily asked.

"Yeah. She told me she met him at Mo's Pub a couple of nights before. He and a friend were there, playing pool, and she thought he was cute, so she asked him to the dance."

"She asked him?" Brodie asked. "He didn't approach her?"

"Not the way she told it." Ruthie shrugged. "That was Renee—she liked calling the shots in a relationship and wasn't afraid to make the first move."

"What did you think of him?" Emily asked.

Ruthie made a face. "I didn't like him. He struck me as too full of himself, and a phony. I told Renee that, too, and she said they had a lot of fun, but she didn't think she'd go out with him again—he wasn't her type. To tell you the truth, it surprised me she went out with him that one time. She generally likes older men who are a little rougher around the edges, you know? Outdoorsmen and daredevils. Alex was close to her age, and far too smooth."

"Did Renee mention anything that might have happened later that night, maybe when Alex took her home—anything that seemed off or upsetting?" Emily asked.

"No. Nothing like that. She just said he wasn't her type. My husband didn't like Alex, either. In fact, he and I left the dance early. I was afraid if Bob had one too many drinks he might end up punching Alex.

Alex kept popping off like he was an authority on everything and I could tell it was getting to Bob."

"You married Bob Schultz?" Emily asked, picturing the rancher's son who had never really been part of their group.

Ruthie smiled, her expression softening. "Yeah. I came home for Christmas after my first semester at Brown and he and I met up at a skating party my church had organized for the youth. We just really hit it off. I ended up transferring to Junction to finish my degree and we got married my sophomore year. We have two kids—Ian is six and Sophia is five."

"Wow," Emily said, trying—and failing—to hide her surprise.

Ruthie laughed. "I know! I was going to save the world and have all these adventures. But marriage and motherhood and running our ranch is adventure enough for me."

"You sound really happy."

"That's because I am." Her expression sobered once more. "Except, of course, I'm worried about Renee."

"Now that we know she's missing, we'll be looking for her," Brodie said. "You gave Travis a description of her vehicle, right?"

Ruthie nodded. "She drives a silver RAV4. Travis said he would put out a bulletin to let law enforcement all over the state know to be on the lookout for her. Maybe they will find her in Junction with some new guy she met." She smiled, but the expression didn't reach her eyes. "That would be just like Renee."

Brodie rose, and the women stood also. "Thank you for talking to me," Emily said.

Ruthie reached out and gripped Emily's wrist. "Be honest with me. Do you think this guy went after Renee?"

"I don't know," Emily said. "He hasn't had a previous relationship with any of the other women he's killed—at least not as far as we know. And all of them have been found very shortly after they were killed—within minutes, even." She gently extricated herself from Ruthie's grasp. "But people aren't always predictable. All I can tell you is that this doesn't follow his pattern so far."

Ruthie nodded. "I know you can't make any promises, but I'm holding out hope that it's just a sick coincidence that she knew this man." She shuddered. "I can't believe we spent a whole evening with him. I thought he was a bit of a jerk, but I never in a million years would have pegged him as a killer."

"If we could do that, we could prevent crimes before they happened," Brodie said. "But we can't."

They walked with Ruthie to the front door, where she offered Emily another hug. "We'll have to get together after this is all over," Ruthie said. "I'd like you to meet my family."

"I'd like that, too," Emily said.

Brodie waited until Ruthie was gone before he spoke. "What do you think?" he asked.

Emily worried her lower lip between her teeth. "Alex went out with Michaela Underwood, too," she said. "So we know he has used asking women out as a way to get to them."

"But he killed Michaela on that first date. Renee Parmenter went out with him at least once and lived to tell the tale."

"That was about a week before he and Tim killed Kelly Farrow and Christy O'Brien," Emily said. "Maybe Alex was still working on his plan, or maybe killing women was still a fantasy for him then."

"She didn't tell her sister about anything unusual happening on the date, but that doesn't mean nothing did," Brodie said. "She might not have wanted to worry her sister."

"If Renee was wary of Alex, she probably wouldn't have gone out with him again," Emily said.

"So you don't think he used a second date as a way to get to her so he could kill her?" Brodie asked.

"I don't know," Emily said. "Maybe he charmed her. Or she was physically attracted to him in spite of her misgivings. Attraction can make people do things they know they shouldn't."

Her eyes met his, hoping he'd get the message that what had happened between them in his cabin yesterday was not going to be repeated. Brodie wasn't a bad person—far from it. But she didn't like the way he made her feel so out of control and not in charge of her decisions.

His gaze slid away from hers. "I hope Alex didn't

murder Renee Parmenter. But I can't say I've got a good feeling about this."

"No, I don't, either," she admitted.

"Have you come up with any ideas about where he might be hiding—or what he intends to do next?"

"No, I haven't."

He clapped her on the back. "Then you'd better get to work. I still think you can give us something useful if you put your mind to it."

"Because of course you're always right."

"I've got good instincts. And so do you, if you'd pay attention to them."

He strode away, leaving her to wonder at his words—and at the look that accompanied them. She and Brodie seemed to specialize in nonverbal communication and mixed messages. It was probably time they cleared the air between them, but coming right out and saying what she felt wasn't something she had had much practice at. Like most people, she liked to protect her feelings. She had allowed herself to be vulnerable to a man exactly once, and the ending made her unwilling to do so again.

BRODIE HAD CLAIMED a desk in the corner of the sheriff's department conference room that had been turned into a situation room. The faces of the victims of the Ice Cold Killer surrounded him as he worked, and the scant evidence collected in the case crowded a row of folding tables against one wall. He hunched over his laptop, scanning databases, trying to trace Renee Parmenter's movements since her disappearance.

Travis had asked Ruth to run a notice in the paper, asking anyone who had any knowledge of Renee's whereabouts to contact the sheriff's department, but that wouldn't appear until tomorrow. As it was, Renee had been missing four days. Brodie feared they might already be too late.

The door to the room opened and Travis entered. He scanned the room, his gaze lingering a moment on the faces of the dead before he shifted his attention to Brodie. "Are you coming up with anything?"

Brodie pushed his chair back from the table that served as his desk. "The report from the CBI profiler came in a few minutes ago," he said.

"And?" Travis asked.

Brodie turned back to the computer, found the file and opened it. "I forwarded the whole thing to you, but the gist of it is, she thinks now that Alex is working alone, and he knows we know his identity, that's increasing the pressure on him. He's likely to kill more often and perhaps take more risks. He's trying to relieve the pressure and attempting to prove to us and to himself that we can't stop him."

"We have to find him in order to stop him," Travis said. "Does the profiler have any idea where he's likely to be hiding?"

"She doesn't mention that," Brodie said. "I'm still hoping Emily will come up with some ideas."

Travis shook his head. "I don't think my sister can

help us with this one. We're going to have to keep looking and hope we catch a break."

"I've been working on trying to track Renee Parmenter," Brodie said. "It looks like she bought gas here in town, charging it to her credit card, the afternoon she disappeared. After that, there's nothing."

"Maybe she ran into Alex at the gas station, or he flagged down her car on the side of the road and she stopped because she recognized him," Travis said. "He asked her to give him a lift and he killed her."

"And then what?" Brodie asked. "Did he hide her car with the body? He's never done that before."

Travis rubbed his chin. "Hiding her doesn't fit with what we know about him, either," he said. "Alex wants us to know he's killed these women— that he got away with another murder. He wants to rub it in our faces that we aren't even slowing him down."

"He and Tim kidnapped Jamie and her sister and planned to kill them later," Brodie said. "Maybe that's a new MO for him."

"They kidnapped Jamie's sister in order to lure Jamie to them," Travis said. "Tim told her they wanted to kill a deputy as a way of getting to me. Fortunately, she was able to fight off Tim until we got to her."

"If Alex did kidnap Renee, he'd have to keep her somewhere," Brodie said. "We should consider that when we're focusing on places he might be hiding."

The phone on Brodie's desk beeped. He picked it up and Adelaide said, "Is the sheriff in there with you?"

"Yes."

"I've got a caller on the line who wants to talk to him. They were pretty insistent that I had to put them through to Travis. They won't give a name and I can't tell if it's a man or a woman."

"You record the incoming calls, right?" Brodie asked.

"Of course."

"Travis is right here." Brodie hit the button to put the call on speaker and handed the handset to Travis.

"Hello? This is Sheriff Walker."

After a second's pause, a wavery voice came on the line. "I saw that girl you're looking for. She was hitchhiking on Dixon Pass. That's a dangerous thing to do, hitchhiking."

Travis's eyes met Brodie's. He could tell the sheriff was thinking the same thing he was—how did the caller know about Renee when the story hadn't even come out yet in the paper? "Who is calling?" Travis asked. "When did you see this hitchhiker?"

"Oh, it was a couple of days ago." The man… woman…sounded frail and uncertain. "I just wanted you to know."

"Could you describe her for me, please?" Travis asked. "And tell me exactly where you saw her."

But the call had already ended. Brodie took the

handset and replaced it. "I'll contact the phone company and see if they can tell us anything about who made the call," he said.

Travis nodded. "I'd bet my next paycheck they don't find anything," he said. "I don't think that was a random Good Samaritan."

"Me, either," Brodie agreed. "Alex Woodruff is used to acting. It might not be too difficult for him to disguise his voice."

"Yes. Maybe he's annoyed that we haven't found Renee's body yet and decided to give us a hint."

"Or maybe he's set a trap."

"Come on," Travis said. "Let's go up to Dixon Pass and find out."

Chapter Ten

On the way up to the pass, Travis called Gage and let him know where they were headed and why. "I don't want the whole department up there in case this is a false alarm," Travis told his brother. "And I also don't put it past Alex to do something like this to draw us away from town. Just be alert if you don't hear from us in twenty minutes or so."

"Will do," Gage said. "But if that was Alex calling to give you a clue as to where to find Renee's body, it was a pretty vague one. Where are you going to look?"

"I have some ideas."

They parked Travis's sheriff's department SUV, which still bore faint traces of Alex's graffiti on the driver's side, at the barricades two-thirds of the way up the pass. They walked the rest of the way, past two dump trucks waiting to carry away loads of snow and an idling front-end loader. Travis stopped at the post that indicated the turnoff to the former ski area, most of the old road now buried under the avalanche that had almost killed Brodie and Gage. "The highway crews were able to clear this section of road pretty quickly," he said. "Apparently, most of the snow that came down was below this point."

"I still wonder what set off the slide," Brodie said. "Gage and I thought we heard a gunshot right before it came down."

"The road crew swears they had nothing to do with it," Travis said. "They were on a break when the avalanche happened. They don't remember seeing anyone around the road who wasn't supposed to be here, either."

Brodie continued to stare down at the river of snow. Sometimes things happened for no discernable reason, but the investigator in him didn't easily accept that.

"Gage said you didn't see anything suspicious down there before the slide," Travis said.

"No. It didn't look like anyone had been around for a while. I didn't see anywhere Alex might have been hiding—though we weren't able to get down there to take a closer look at the buildings. But if we couldn't get down there, neither could Alex, so I'd rule him out."

"Let's find someone to talk to about Renee Parmenter." They set out walking again. When they rounded the next curve, they could see a wall of blinding white, easily fifteen feet high, obliterating the roadway. A massive rotary snowblower was slowly chewing its way through the wall, sending a great plume of snow into the canyon below.

A man in a hard hat, blaze-orange vest over his parka, approached. "What can I do for you officers?" he asked.

"We're looking for a missing woman," Travis said.

The man scratched his head under the hard hat. "We haven't seen any women around here."

"What about cars?" Brodie asked. "Do you ever come across cars buried under these avalanches?"

"Sometimes. But we usually know they're there going in because someone reports it. If there was a driver or passenger in the vehicle, emergency services would have already worked to dig them out, and they usually flag the car for us so we can work around it. Hitting one could wreck a plow, but our guys watch out. There are all kinds of hazards that come down with the slides—rocks, trees. Once we found a dead elk."

"You might want to keep an eye out for a car up here," Travis said.

"What makes you think your missing woman is up here?" the man asked.

"We got a call," Travis said. "She's been missing since Monday—before the slide."

The man nodded. "Okay. We'll keep our eyes open."

He walked away and Travis and Brodie stood for a few minutes longer, watching the steady progress of the blower, until Brodie's ears rang with the sounds of the machinery. "Let's get out of here!" he shouted to be heard above the din. The noise, the endless snow and the eeriness of a highway with no traffic were beginning to get to him. Or maybe he was just twitchy after almost being buried alive in an avalanche.

Back in Travis's SUV, the sheriff didn't immediately start the vehicle. "If Alex killed Renee Parmenter, I have to believe he chose her because she knew him and was inclined to trust him," he said. "He took advantage of their previous relationship."

"Same with Denise Switcher," Brodie said. "She knew him from the university, so was more likely to stop when he flagged her down. He doesn't have Tim to help him lure and subdue his victims, so he's searching for easier prey—women who are more inclined to trust him."

Travis turned to Brodie. "Who else does he know who might trust him?" he asked. "Answer that question and we might be able to figure out who his next victim will be."

"We could start by interviewing single women in town, find out who else he—or Tim—might have dated in the weeks they've been here," Brodie said.

"Emily mentioned a woman he dated in Fort Collins," Travis said. "She dropped him because he wanted to strangle her while they were having sex."

Brodie scowled. "Maybe he planned to keep on choking her until she was dead." The more he learned about Alex, the greater his urgency to stop him.

"I'll ask to dig a little deeper. Maybe he had another girlfriend who came here for a visit and we haven't heard about her yet." He started the SUV and pulled out to turn around. But before he could make the turn, the man in the hard hat and orange vest ran toward them, waving his arms. Travis stopped and rolled down his window. "What is it?" he asked.

The man stopped beside the SUV, hands on his knees, panting. "We…found something," he gasped. "A car. And there's a woman inside."

"Poor Ruth." Emily's first thought on hearing of Renee Parmenter's death was of her sister. Yes, Renee had suffered at the hands of a murderer, but Ruth had to live with the knowledge that the person she loved had been taken so brutally. "I guess there's no doubt Renee was murdered?"

"No," Travis said. "She was killed just like the others."

"Alex even left his Ice Cold calling card," Brodie said. He and Travis flanked Emily on the living room sofa. A fire crackled in the woodstove across from them and a pile of wedding gifts that had been delivered when the road reopened waited on a table against the wall. Everything looked so ordinary and peaceful, which made the news of Renee's murder all the more disorienting.

"Have you told Ruth yet?" Emily asked.

"No," Travis said. "I was on my way there after I talked to you."

"I want to go with you," she said. "Maybe it will make it a little easier on her if she has a friend there."

"I was hoping you'd say that," Travis said. He stood. "Let's go see Ruth. If we wait too long, she might hear about this from someone else, and we don't want that."

By the time Ruth answered Travis's knock, Emily could see she had prepared herself for the worst. Her gaze slid past Emily and fixed on Travis. "Have you found her?" she asked, her voice tight, as if she had to force the words out.

"May we come in?" he asked.

She stepped back to let them pass. The house was an older one, with nineties-era blond wood and brass fixtures, the room cluttered with toys and shoes and a pile of laundry on one end of the sofa. A large window looked out onto pastures and hayfields, now covered with snow. "The kids are in school and my husband is out checking fences," Ruth said as she led the way to the sofa. She moved a child's book off the sofa and picked up a pillow from the floor, then sat, holding the pillow in her lap. "Tell me what you've found. It can't be anything worse than I've already imagined."

Travis removed his hat and sat across from Ruth while Emily settled in next to her. "We found your sister's body at the top of Dixon Pass, in her car," Travis said. "She was murdered—probably by Alex Woodruff."

Ruth made a short, sharp sound and covered her

mouth with her hand. Emily took her other hand and squeezed it. Ruth held on tightly and uncovered her mouth. "When?" she asked.

"The car was buried by the avalanche that closed the road on Tuesday morning," Travis said. "She was killed before then."

Ruth closed her eyes, visibly pulling herself together. "Is there someone you'd like me to call?" Emily asked. "Your husband, or a friend?"

"Bob will be in soon." She opened her eyes, which shone with unshed tears. "If you know who did this, why don't you arrest him and stop him?" she asked.

"When we find Alex, we'll arrest him," Travis said. "Do you have any idea where he might be hiding? That night you and your husband met him, did he say anything at all that might give us a clue?"

She shook her head. "I'm sorry. We talked about school and the dance and the weather—just ordinary small talk among people who didn't know each other well."

"And you're sure Renee never mentioned seeing or talking to him after that night?" Travis asked.

"No. I really don't think she heard from him or saw him after that one date," Ruth said.

"You said you didn't like him," Travis said. "Maybe knowing that, she decided not to talk about him."

"Renee wasn't like that," Ruth said. "If she liked someone and I didn't, she would have made a point of mentioning him, just to give me a hard time." She shook her head. "She was really definite about not wanting to see him again. If he had called and asked her out again, she would have been on the phone to me as soon as she hung up with him." Her breath caught, and she swallowed, then added, her voice fainter, "That's how we were. We talked about everything."

"I'm very sorry for your loss," Travis said. He stood, hat in hand. "Once the medical examiner has completed his autopsy, we'll release the body to the funeral home of your choice. Call my office if you have any questions."

Ruth stood and walked with them to the door. "Are you sure you don't want me to stay until your husband gets here?" Emily asked.

"I'll be okay." She took a shuddering breath. "I do better with this kind of stuff on my own—but thank you."

Emily squeezed her arm. "Call me if you need anything. Or if you just want to talk."

Ruth nodded, then looked at Travis again. "You'll find him and stop him, won't you?" she asked, the words more plea than query.

"Yes," he said.

He and Emily didn't say anything until they were almost back to the sheriff's department. "Denise was killed the same day," Emily said. "Right before the avalanche. And her car was found at the top of the pass."

"The first two murders—Kelly Farrow and Christy O'Brien—happened within hours of each other," Travis said.

"I think he gets a charge out of getting away with not one, but two killings," Emily said.

"The profiler from the Colorado Bureau of Investigation said he's feeling more pressure from us now that we know his identity," Travis said. "She believes he'll continue to kill, as a way to relieve the pressure."

Emily nodded. "Yes, that sounds right. And he wants to prove that he can still get away with the crimes—that you'll never catch him."

"He's by himself," Travis said. "Wherever he's hiding can't be that comfortable. We're doing everything we can to alert other people that he's dangerous, so he can't move safely around town, or rely on others for help. He's going to run out of victims he can fool also. We're going to run him to ground."

"I've been thinking," Emily said. "Maybe I can help you find him."

"Have you thought of someplace he might be hiding?"

"No. But he knows me. Maybe I could lure him out of hiding by agreeing to meet him."

"No." Travis didn't look at her, but the muscles along his jaw tightened.

"I'm serious," she said. Her brother wasn't the only stubborn member of this family. "I've lost too many friends to this man. I'll do whatever I can to stop him." Alex was a killer, but she knew him. Maybe she could get to him when no one else could.

Chapter Eleven

"Over my dead body."

So what if it was a cliché? Brodie thought, as soon as he had uttered those words. Travis's announcement that Emily wanted to try to lure Alex to her had prompted a visceral reaction that went beyond coherent speech. The thought of her anywhere near that monster made his blood freeze.

"I already told her the idea was out of the question," Travis said.

"It's a stupid idea." Brodie dropped into the chair across from Travis's desk at the sheriff's department, not sure if his legs were steady enough yet for him to remain standing. "What makes her think he'd come anywhere near her?"

"She fits the profile of the other women he's murdered," Travis said. "Alex knows her. And she's my sister. He's made it clear he enjoys getting back at me and my department—it's why he went after Jamie."

"How can you even look at this logically?" Brodie groused. "She's your sister."

"I made it clear it wasn't going to happen," he said.

"We don't even know where he is," Brodie said. "What was she going to do—put an ad in the paper asking him to meet her? He'd see that as a trap right away."

"Maybe. Or maybe he'd be too tempted by the chance to get at her."

Brodie glared at the sheriff. "You've actually considered this, haven't you? You've run all the possibilities through your head."

Travis shifted in his chair. "It's not going to happen," he said again. "But if anyone is to blame for her coming up with the idea, it's you."

"Me?"

"You're the one who asked her to help with the case. You gave her the idea that she knows Alex better than anyone, and that her insight could help."

"Insight. Her thoughts. I never meant for her to put her life on the line—or anything close to it."

"I know. And I know she really wants to help. But this isn't the way to do it."

Brodie slid down farther in his chair. "I think this case is getting to us all."

Deputy Dwight Prentice stopped in the doorway to the office. "Abel Crutchfield just called in with a tip we ought to check out," he said.

"Who is Abel Crutchfield?" Brodie asked.

"He's a retired guy, spends a lot of time ice fishing in the area," Travis said. "He was the first one to report a blonde woman hanging around near where

Michaela Underwood was murdered. That woman turned out to be Tim Dawson in disguise."

Brodie nodded and sat up straighter. "What's the tip?"

"He says he saw smoke coming from some caves over by Eagle Creek," Dwight said. "Like someone was camping up there. He figured we might want to check it out."

"Take Brodie over there with you and have a look," Travis said. "But call for backup if it looks like anyone is up there."

"Right." Brodie rose. "Much as I'd like to get hold of this guy, better not try to do it by ourselves."

"We should be able to get a good look from across the way," Dwight said. "Enough to see if it's worth going in. Maybe Abel just saw snow blowing off trees and mistook it for smoke."

The drive to Eagle Creek took twenty minutes, most of it on narrow, snow-packed forest service roads. "It doesn't look as if anyone lives out here," Brodie said, staring out at the landscape of snowy woodland.

"They don't," Dwight said. "This is all forest service land. A few snowmobilers or cross-country skiers use the road, and ice fishermen like Abel."

"Sounds like a good place for someone to hide out if he didn't want to be seen," Brodie said.

The caves themselves sat above the river in a limestone formation, centuries of dripping water having hollowed out the rock to form the openings. "Most of these caves are pretty shallow," Dwight said as he led the way through the snow along the riverbank. "There are only a couple that are deep enough to provide any real shelter."

"Deep enough to live in?" Brodie asked.

"Maybe. It wouldn't be very comfortable. You'd have to have a fire to keep from freezing to death, and there would be a lot of smoke and dampness. Not to mention bats, bugs and wild animals."

"It doesn't sound like Alex Woodruff's kind of place," Brodie said. "He struck me as someone who likes his creature comforts."

"Yeah, but he's desperate now. He can't be as choosy."

They halted on a bench of land across the river from the largest opening. Dwight dug out a pair of binoculars and trained them on the cave. "The snow around the opening is churned up," he said. "Someone—or something—has been going in and out of there." He shifted the binoculars. "And there's a definite path leading up there."

Brodie sniffed the air. "I can smell smoke—like a campfire."

Dwight handed him the binoculars. "There's no smoke coming from there right now."

Brodie focused the glasses on the cave opening. It was impossible to see into the dark space, but there was definitely no movement at the entrance. He returned the binoculars to Dwight. "What do you think we should do now?"

"I'd like to get a little closer before we call in the cavalry," Dwight said. "We can approach from below and anyone inside wouldn't be able to see us until we were almost on him."

"Sounds good to me."

It took twenty minutes to retrace their steps along the river, negotiating over icy rock and snow-covered deadfall. They had to walk farther downstream to find a place to cross—a bridge of felled trees that required stepping carefully and balancing like a tight-rope walker. But when they reached the other side, they found the worn path through the snow that they had glimpsed from the other side.

Weapons drawn, they moved cautiously up the path. The rushing water tumbling over rocks and downed trees drowned out all other sound. Dwight took the lead, while Brodie covered him, staying several yards behind. They reached a series of rock steps that led up to the cave and halted. "Let me go up first, while you stay down here," Dwight whispered. "I should be able to get right up on the entrance without being seen. You come up after me and we'll flank the entrance and demand whoever is in there to come out. If we don't get an answer, we'll shine a light in, maybe try to draw his fire."

Brodie agreed and Dwight started up, keeping close to the cliff side, placing each step carefully, the rush of the water below drowning out his approach. When he was safely up the steps and stationed on the left side of the cave entrance, he motioned for Brodie to follow.

Brodie moved up more quickly and took up a position on the opposite side of the cave entrance. "Is anyone in there?" Dwight called.

The words bounced off the canyon walls and echoed back at them, but no sound came from the cave.

"This is the Rayford County Sheriff's Department!" Dwight called. "You need to come out with your hands up!"

No answer or movement. Dwight unsnapped his flashlight from his utility belt and trained the powerful beam into the cave entrance. A rock fire ring sat about two feet inside, full of dark ash and a couple of pieces of charred wood. Brodie stooped, picked up a rock and tossed it inside the cave. It bounced off the stone floor and rolled toward the back, then all was silent again.

Dwight's eyes met Brodie's. He jerked his head toward the cave and indicated he was going in. Brodie nodded. Instincts could be wrong, but it didn't feel to him as if anyone was in there. Dwight swung the flashlight in ahead of him, then entered the cave, staying close to the wall. He had to duck to enter. Weapon ready, Brodie watched him disappear from sight.

"Come on in!" Dwight called a few seconds later. "There's no one in here."

Brodie unhooked his own flashlight and followed

Dwight into the cave. He swept the light over the mostly empty space, coming to rest on a pile of garbage in the corner—tin cans, beer bottles and food wrappers. He moved closer to the fire. "Someone was here for a while," he said. "And not that long ago."

"The ashes in the firepit are still warm." Dwight crouched beside the rock ring and held his hand over the charred wood.

Brodie holstered his gun and played the flashlight over the scuffed dirt on the floor of the cave. The space was maybe ten feet deep and eight feet wide, tall enough to stand up in, but barely, with a ceiling of smoke-blackened rock and a dirt floor. It smelled of smoke, stale food and animal droppings. "Not exactly the Ritz," he said.

"No one would be camping here in the middle of winter unless he had to," Dwight said. "It has to be Alex."

Brodie trained his light on the garbage pile again. "He's buying food somewhere." He nudged a beer bottle with his toe. "Lots of craft beer, chips and canned pasta."

"That sounds like a college guy's diet," Dwight said.

"If he's shopping, someone in Eagle Mountain must have seen him," Brodie said. "Why haven't they reported him to the sheriff's department?"

"He could be breaking into summer cabins,"

Dwight said. "Or shopping at the grocery store wearing a disguise."

"If he was here this morning, it doesn't look as if he intends to return," Brodie said. "There's no sleeping bag, no stash of food—not even any firewood."

"We'll watch the place for a couple of days, see if he comes back," Dwight said. "But I agree—it looks like he's cleared out. Maybe he saw Abel looking up this way and decided to leave."

"There's not much here, but we'd better look through it, see if we can find anything significant," Brodie said. He smoothed on a pair of gloves and began sifting through the garbage, while Dwight examined the firepit. He combed through half a dozen beer bottles, two empty ravioli cans, several candy bar wrappers and two chip bags, but found nothing that told them where Alex might be now. They took photographs and bagged everything as evidence. They might be able to get DNA off the beer bottles that would prove Alex was the person who had hidden in this cave, but Brodie didn't see how that would be useful in their case against him.

"I may have found something," Dwight said. He used a pen to lift something from the ashes and held it aloft. Brodie recognized the coiled binding of a pocket-size notebook. "The cover is gone, and the edge of the pages are charred, but most of it's intact," Dwight said. He spread the notebook on the ground and Brodie joined him in leaning over it. Dwight flipped through the pages, which appeared to contain everything from grocery lists—*chips, lunch meat, cookies, soda, razor*—to cryptic numbers and calculations. Most of the pages were blank.

"We'll have to go through this at the office and see if there's anything significant," Dwight said. He reached into his coat and pulled out a plastic evidence bag.

Brodie continued to flip through the pages. He found what looked like phone numbers, notes on what might have been climbing routes, then stopped on a page that was simply a column of letters—*KF, CO, FW, LG, AA, MU, TP, DD, JD, LW, RP, DS, EW.*

"What have you got there?" Dwight asked. "Are they some kind of abbreviations? For what?"

Brodie repeated the letters under his breath, then stopped in mid-syllable as the realization of what they represented hit him. "They're initials," he said. "Of all the women he's killed."

"Kelly Farrow, Christy O'Brien, Fiona Winslow, Lauren Grenado, Anita Allbritton, Michaela Underwood, Lynn Wallace, Renee Parmenter and Denise Switcher," Dwight said. "There's a line through *TP*—Tammy Patterson. She got away from him. Another line through *DD* and *JD*—Donna and Jamie Douglas. They escaped, too."

"They're in order of the attacks," Brodie said. "He must have killed Renee before Denise." He frowned at the last letters on the page. "Who is *EW*?"

"Is there a victim we haven't found yet?" Dwight asked. "Or someone he's gone after today?"

Brodie stood, his stomach heaving and a chill sweeping through him. "*EW* could be Emily Walker." He clapped Dwight on the shoulder and shoved the notebook toward him. "Bag that and let's get out of here. We have to make sure Emily is all right."

Chapter Twelve

"I'm fine, and I think you're both overreacting." Emily had been up to her eyeballs in surveys to review when Brodie and Travis had burst in on her late Friday afternoon, demanding to know what she was doing and if she had talked to or seen Alex Woodruff. "Alex hasn't been anywhere near here, and as for what I'm doing, I'm working. And I don't need you interrupting."

"You could be in danger," Brodie said. "Promise me you won't go anywhere without me or Travis or Gage with you."

"What are you talking about?" She turned to Travis. "Why are you both here this time of day? What's happened?"

Travis pulled a plastic evidence envelope from his coat and held it out to her. "Brodie and Dwight found this in a cave over by Eagle Creek," he said. "We think it belongs to Alex."

She studied the half-charred notebook, and the

list of letters inscribed on the page in front of her. "What does this have to do with me?"

"The letters on that page are the initials of the women Alex killed," he said. His face was pale and drawn, like a man in pain. "The crossed-out letters are the three women who got away."

She read through the list again and nodded. "All right. I can see that."

"The last letters are *EW*," Brodie said. He put a hand on her shoulder. "Emily Walker."

This announcement elicited an astonished laugh from her. "*EW* could stand for anything," she said. "Ellen White. Elaine Wilson—there are a lot of women with those initials."

"What were those names again?" Brodie had pulled out a notebook and pen and was poised to write. "We'll need to check on those women, as well."

She shifted in her seat. "I don't actually know any women with those names," Emily said. "I was just giving you examples of women's names with those initials."

"We'll research tax rolls and any other records we can find for women with the initials *EW*," Travis said. "But we wanted to be sure you're all right."

"I'm fine." Some of her annoyance receded, replaced by a cold undercurrent of fear. She thought Brodie and Travis were overreacting—but what if they weren't? "I'm smart enough to stay far away from Alex Woodruff," she said.

"Last I heard, you were volunteering to lure him to you," Brodie said.

"I did. But Travis persuaded me that was a bad idea." She shrugged. "It wouldn't work without the sheriff's department's cooperation. I mean, I'm not misguided enough to try to do something like that without a whole bunch of law enforcement watching my back."

Some of the tension went out of his shoulders. "I'm relieved you're all right," he said.

His real concern for her touched her, so that she had to look away. She focused on Travis. "I'm fine. It was sweet of you to worry, but don't."

"What are you doing the rest of the day?" Brodie asked.

She really wanted to tell him that was none of his business, but that would only lead to another argument. The man never took no for an answer. "Since the favors for the wedding didn't get here while the highway was open, a bunch of us are getting together with Lacy in a little while to make everything she needs. We're going to do crafts, drink wine, eat a lot of good things and stay right here on the ranch."

"Good." Travis tucked the evidence bag back into his pocket. "Don't say anything about this to anyone."

She shook her head. "Of course not."

"Come on, Brodie. Let's see about those other women."

They turned to leave, but she stopped them. "Did you say you found that in a cave?" she asked.

Travis nodded. "It looked like Alex had spent at least a couple of nights there, though he isn't there now. We've got a reserve deputy watching the place, in case he returns."

She wrinkled her nose. "That doesn't sound very comfortable—not like Alex."

"We agree," Brodie said. "It shows how desperate he's getting. The pressure on him is increasing."

"Then he's liable to become even more violent and unpredictable," she said.

"He's more likely to make mistakes," Travis said. "We're going to take advantage of that."

"Be careful," she said, but the two men were already turning away again.

She tried to put their visit, and the disturbing news about the list of initials, out of her mind and return her focus to the student surveys. But that proved impossible. She kept repeating the names of the murdered women, and picturing that *EW* at the bottom of the list. Surely that didn't stand for Emily Walker, but the idea that it *might* definitely shook her.

Travis and Brodie and Gage and her family and friends and everyone else she knew would protect her. They formed a living barricade between her body and anyone who might try to harm her. But could they really keep Alex away? He had proved so sly and elusive, slipping in and out of crime scenes unseen, leaving scarcely a trace of evidence. Every law enforcement officer in the county had been tracking him for weeks, yet they hadn't even touched him. Could he somehow get past all her defenses and take her down when she least expected it?

She shuddered and pushed the thought away. Alex wasn't a mythical boogeyman who could walk through walls. He was flesh and blood and as vulnerable as anyone. And she was safe. She was smart and wary and protected by all those who loved her.

She didn't believe Brodie loved her—not in the way she had once wanted him to. But she believed he would protect her. He might be glibly charming and socially superficial at times, but he took his duty as an officer of the law seriously. She tried to take comfort from that.

She was grateful when Lacy came to her and asked for help setting up for their get-together with the other women in the wedding party. "This is so nice of everyone to help," Lacy said as she and Emily and Bette set out craft supplies and readied the refreshments.

"You deserve every bit of help we can give," Bette said, arranging paintbrushes at each place setting down the long dining room table, which had been spread with brown paper to protect its polished wood surface. "Besides, this is going to be fun."

At six o'clock, the other women began arriving: Lacy's mother and all the bridesmaids—Brenda Prentice, Gage's wife, Maya Renfro, and Paige Riddell—as well as wedding guests veterinarian Darcy Marsh, Deputy Jamie Douglas and her sister, Donna. Along with Emily, Travis's mom and Bette, they made a lively party. "We're going to be decorating fancy sugar cookies," Bette explained, passing a plate of cookies shaped liked butterflies and birds. "We're using colored frosting that's the consistency of paint. Use your paintbrushes to decorate the cookies however you wish. When the cookies are dry, we'll package them up with fancy wrappings."

"I'm not very artistic," Jamie said, looking doubtful. "What if my cookies turn out ugly?"

"Then we can eat them," Donna said, sending a ripple of laughter around the table.

"I don't know," Maya said. "That might be an incentive to mess up."

"They'll turn out great," Bette said. "And when we're done, we have more cookies and plenty of other yummy party food."

Emily dipped her paintbrush in a small pot of yellow icing and began to decorate a butterfly. Though she had never considered herself an artist, the results of her efforts pleased her. "Everyone is going to love these," she said.

"Probably more than the drink cozies and pens I ordered," Lacy said. She held up a purple hummingbird. "I kind of like the reminder of spring amid all this snow."

"The weather is breaking all kinds of records this year," Darcy said. "Ryder says no one he works with can remember the highway closing so often and for so long due to avalanches and the sheer volume of snow."

"The science classes have been measuring snow amounts and tracking the weather data," Maya, a high school teacher, said. "Word is forecasts look promising for a shift in the weather to a drier pattern. That will give the snow time to settle and the highway department to get the roads in good shape to stay open."

"That's good news." Emily turned to Lacy. "You shouldn't have any trouble getting away for your honeymoon."

"Travis has to catch the Ice Cold Killer first," Lacy said. "He'll never leave town with the case still open. I'll be lucky to drag him to the altar for a few hours."

"We're getting close," Jamie said. "Now that we have a good idea who the killer is, we have everyone in the county looking for him. Someone is going to see Alex and tip us off in time to arrest him."

"I just pray they find him before he kills someone else," Bette said. The others murmured agreement.

"Do any of you know a woman in town with the initials *EW*?" Emily asked. She had promised not to tell anyone about the notebook with Alex's supposed list—but that didn't mean she couldn't do a little digging of her own.

"You mean besides you?" Lacy asked. "Why?"

She shrugged. "No reason. Just wondering."

"That's not the kind of question a person asks for no reason," Brenda said. "What's going on? Does this have something to do with Alex?"

Emily grappled for some plausible story. "I, um, saw the initials in graffiti on the bathroom stall at Mo's Pub," she said. "I was just curious." She hoped the others didn't think the story was as lame as it sounded to her.

"There's Ellie Watkins," Maya said. "But she's only six—a classmate of my niece, Casey. So I don't think anyone would be writing about her on bathroom walls."

"Elaine Wulf is one of the museum volunteers," said Brenda, who managed the local history museum. "But she's at least eighty and I can't think she'd have been up to anything that would warrant writing about it on a bathroom wall."

The others laughed and Emily forced a weak smile. "It was probably only a tourist, then. Never mind."

"What did the message say?" Lacy asked. "It must have been pretty juicy if you're asking about it now."

"Oh, it was nothing." She held up her finished butterfly. "What do you think?"

They all complimented her and began showing off their own work, but Emily was aware of Lacy eyeing her closely.

When the women took a break to eat, Lacy pulled Emily aside. "What is going on?" she asked. "What was all that about a woman with the initials *EW*? And don't give me that lame story about graffiti in the restroom at Mo's Pub. There is no graffiti there. Mo wouldn't allow it."

Emily chewed her lip. "You have to promise not to let Travis know I told you this," she said.

"I can keep a secret—within reason."

"Dwight and Brodie checked out a cave where Alex might have been camping. They found a half-burned notebook in the fire ring. In it was a list of initials that matched the initials of all the women he's killed—or attempted to kill. The last set of initials on the list was *EW.*"

Lacy's face paled. "Emily Walker—you!"

"It's not me!" Emily protested. "I mean, I'm not dead, and Alex hasn't tried to get to me, so it must be someone else. I was trying to figure out who it might be."

"I'm sure Travis is looking for her, too."

"Of course he is. I just thought with a room full of women here, someone might know a woman with those initials that Travis could check on—just to make sure she's all right."

Lacy rubbed her hands up and down her arms. "I hate to think the killer is out there stalking another woman."

"And I hate that I've upset you." Emily put her arm around her friend. "Come on. Let's go back to the others and do our best not to think about this anymore. Think about your wedding and how wonderful it's going to be when you and Travis are married."

For the rest of the evening, Emily did her best to put Alex out of her mind. She ate and drank, and listened as the married women in the group told stories of their own weddings—Travis's father had apparently been late to the altar because he got lost on the way to the church, and Lacy's father had proposed by hiding an engagement ring in a piece of cheesecake... and her mother had almost swallowed it.

After they ate, Bette led them in making wedding-themed wreaths to hang on all the outside doors of the ranch house, as well as the doors of the four guest cabins. They wrapped grapevine wreaths in white tulle and silver ribbon and added glittered snowflakes and feathers. The end result was surprisingly delicate and beautiful.

They wrapped the cookies and placed them in baskets, to be handed out at the wedding in two days. "They look like little works of art," Maya said.

"Definitely too pretty to eat," Brenda said.

"You have to eat them," Bette said. "They're delicious."

"They were!" Donna said. She, like everyone else, had eaten her share of "mistakes."

After everyone had left, Emily volunteered to help Bette hang the wreaths. "I'll get the cabins, if you'll do the doors in the house," she said, draping four of the wreaths over one arm.

The four guest cabins sat between the house and the barn, along a stone path through the snow. The porch lights of each cabin cast golden pools across the drifted snow, islands in the darkness that she headed for, the chill night air stinging her cheeks and turning her breath into frosty clouds around her head. Emily hung a wreath on each door, smiling at how festive each one looked. The last cabin in the row—the one farthest from the house—was where Brodie was staying. Emily approached it quietly, not anxious to disturb him. He'd been hovering over her even more than her brothers and all the attention made her uncomfortable. The sooner the case was solved and the wedding was over, the better for all of them. Brodie could go back to Denver, she'd return to Fort Collins and everyone could go about life as it had been before.

She hooked the wreath on the nail in the cabin's door and stepped back to make sure it wasn't crooked. Satisfied, she started to turn away, but the door opened and Brodie reached out and took hold of her arm. "Come inside," he said. "We need to talk."

She could have argued that she didn't want to talk to him, but arguing with Brodie never went well. He was too stubborn and determined to be right. If he had something he wanted to say to her, she might as well hear him out now. And then she'd make him listen to a few things she needed to say, too.

Once inside, he released his hold on her and she sat in the room's single chair, while he settled on the side of the bed. He didn't say anything right away, merely looked at her—or rather, looked through her, as if he was searching for some unspoken message in her face. "What did you want to talk about?" she asked, forcing herself to sit still and not fidget.

"Why did you turn down my proposal?" he asked.

She frowned. "Your proposal?"

"I asked you to marry me and you said no."

She couldn't have been more stunned if he had slapped her. "Brodie, that was five years ago."

"Yes, and it's been eating at me ever since. I figured it was past time we cleared the air between us."

Maybe he thought that was a good idea, but did she? Was she ready to share with Brodie all she'd been through—and maybe find out he'd known about her troubles all along? That he had received the letter she had sent to him, and chosen not to get involved? She pressed her lips together, searching for the right words. "I turned you down because I wasn't ready to get married yet—and neither were you."

"You said you loved me."

"I did! But marriage takes more than love. I was only nineteen—I had so many other things I needed to do first."

"What other things?"

Maybe he should have asked these questions five years ago, but he was asking them now, and maybe answering them would help her put herself back in that time and her mind-set then. "I was only a sophomore in college. I knew I needed to finish my education and get established in my career before I married."

"Why? Lots of people get married while they're still in school. I wouldn't have held you back."

"You would have, even if you didn't intend to." She shifted in her chair, trying to find the words to make him see. "You know my family places a lot of value on education and being successful in whatever you choose to do," she said.

"I think most families are like that," he said.

"Yes, but mine especially so. My mother has a PhD, did you know that? In entomology. And my father has built the Walking W into one of the largest and most successful ranches in the state. Travis is the youngest sheriff our county has ever had, and Gage is a decorated officer with a wall full of commendations."

"I wouldn't have held you back," he said again.

"You were established in a job that could require you to move across the state at any time," she said. "In fact, you did move, right after we broke up."

"The department takes spouse's jobs into consideration," he said, for all the world as if he was making an argument all over again for her to marry him.

"You weren't ready to settle down," she said. "Not really."

"How do you know?" he asked.

She straightened. Why not come out and say what she had been thinking? "If you really loved me so much, you would have tried harder to persuade me to accept your proposal. Instead, after I said no, you simply walked away."

He stood and began to pace, his boot heels striking hard on the wood floor. "Did you really expect me to browbeat you into changing your decision—or worse, to beg?" He raked a hand through his hair and whirled to face her. "Did you ever think that I didn't walk away because I didn't love you, but because I respected you enough to know your own mind?"

His words—and the emotion behind them—hit her like a blow, knocking the breath from her. "I...I still don't think we were ready to marry," she managed to stammer. "So many other things could have happened to tear us apart."

"Like what?" His gaze burned into her, daring her to look away. "What would be so bad our love wouldn't have been enough to overcome it?"

She wet her lips and pushed on. "What if I'd gotten pregnant?"

"We'd have been careful, taken precautions."

"We didn't always do that before, did we?"

He stared at her, and she saw doubt crowd out defiance. He studied her, eyes full of questions. "Emily, is there something you're not telling me?" he asked, his voice so low she had to lean forward to catch all his words.

She was not going to cry. If she started, she might never stop. "I told you I wrote to you after you moved," she said, speaking slowly and carefully.

"And I told you, I never received your letter." He sank onto the edge of the bed once more, as if his legs would no longer support him. "Did you really think I would ignore you?"

"I didn't know. I didn't know what to think."

"What did the letter say?"

She sighed. Did this really matter now? It did to

her—but would it to him? "After you left, I found out I was pregnant," she said.

"Emily." Just her name, said so softly, with such tenderness and sorrow the sound almost broke her. She blinked furiously, but couldn't hold back the tears. "My parents, of course, were very upset. Travis was furious. He's the one who insisted I contact you, though at first I refused."

"Why didn't you want me to know?" he asked. "I would have done the right thing. I already wanted to marry you."

"That's exactly why I didn't want you to know," she said. "I was going to have a baby, but I still didn't want to be married. And I didn't want you to marry me because you had to. It felt like I was trapping you into something I couldn't believe was right for either one of us."

He leaned forward and took her hand, his fingers warm and gentle as he wrapped them around her palm. "What happened to the baby?" He swallowed. "To our baby?"

"I'm getting to that." She took a deep breath, steadying herself, but not pulling away from him. "My father finally persuaded me that you had a right to know you were going to be a father. So I tried to call and your number had changed. I wrote and the first letter came back, so Travis got your information from the CBI. The second letter didn't come back. I thought that meant you'd received it and decided to ignore it."

"I never would have ignored it." He moved from the bed to his knees in front of her. "I wouldn't ignore you."

"I was going to try to contact you again, but then…" She swallowed again. "Then I lost the baby."

He said nothing, only squeezed her hand and put his other hand on her knee.

She closed her eyes, the sadness and confusion and, yes, relief of those days rising up in her once more like water filling a well. "The doctor said it wasn't anything I'd done—that these things just happen sometimes. I was sad, but relieved, too. I went back to school and went on with my life. We…we never talked about what had happened again."

"Did Gage know this?" he asked, thinking of his conversation with Gage at the bonfire.

She shook her head. "No. He was away at school and then summer school. He knew that something had happened with us, but he never knew about the baby. Just my parents and Travis. I— It felt easier, the fewer people who knew."

"I would have wanted to know." He stroked her arm. "I would have wanted to be there for you."

She nodded, crying quietly now, more comforted by his sympathy than she could have imagined.

"No wonder Travis insists on keeping everything strictly business between us. He thinks I deserted you and our baby when you needed me most." He looked her in the eye, his gaze searching. "I wouldn't have done that, Emily. Never in a million years. I'm sick, hearing about this now."

She put her hand on his shoulder. "I believe that now," she said. Now that she had seen the real pain in his eyes. "I'm glad you know the truth. But we can't go back and change the past. Both of us are different people now."

"Different," he said. "Yet the same." His eyes locked to hers and she felt a surge of emotion, like a wave crashing over her. Brodie still attracted her as no other man ever had. But she was no longer the naive, trusting girl she had been five years ago. She didn't believe in fairy tales, or that either she or Brodie were perfect for each other.

But she did believe in perfect moments, and seizing them. She leaned toward him, and he welcomed her into his arms. She closed her eyes and pressed her lips to his, losing herself in sensation—the scent of him, herbal soap and warm male; the reassuring strength of him, holding her so securely; the taste of him, faintly salty, as she broke the kiss to trace her tongue along his throat.

"I don't want to let you go just yet," he said.

"I'm not going anywhere." She kissed him again, arching her body to his.

"Stay with me tonight," he murmured, his lips caressing her ear.

"Yes." She began to unbutton his shirt, kissing each inch of skin as it was exposed, peeling back the fabric to expose muscular shoulders and a perfectly sculpted chest. She pressed her lips over one taut nipple and he groaned, then dragged her away and began tugging at her clothes.

She laughed as he fumbled with her bra strap. "I never could get the hang of these things," he muttered as she pushed his hands away and removed the garment herself.

Together, they finished undressing and moved to the bed, where they lay facing each other, hands and eyes exploring. "You're even more beautiful than I remember," he said as he traced the curve of her hip.

"Mmm." She kissed her way along his shoulder, smiling to herself as she thought that he was exactly as she remembered him—strong and male and exciting. He slid his hands up her thighs, calluses dragging on her smooth skin. The heat of his fingers pressed into her soft flesh, and into the wetness between her legs.

He leaned into her, the hard ridge of his erection against her stomach making her gasp. He caught the sound in his mouth, his lips closing hungrily over hers, his fingers moving higher, parting her hot folds.

She squirmed and moaned, the sound muffled by the liquid heat of his tongue tangling with her own. He dipped his head to kiss her breasts—butterfly touches of his lips over and around the swelling flesh—then latched onto her sensitive, distended nipple, sucking hard, the pulling sensation reaching all the way to her groin, where she tightened around his plunging finger.

He slid his finger out of her and gripped her

thighs, spreading her wide, cool air rushing across her hot, wet flesh, sending a fresh wave of arousal through her. "What do you want?" he whispered, his voice rough, as if he was fighting for control.

"I want you."

He leaned across her and jerked open the drawer of the bedside table. When he returned, he had a condom packet in his hand. He ripped it open with his teeth and smoothed on the sheath, then pushed her gently onto her back. "Are you ready?"

She nodded. More than ready.

He drove hard, but held her so gently, his fingers stroking, caressing, even as his hips pumped. The sensation of him filling her, stretching her, moving inside her, made her dizzy. "Don't stop," she gasped. "Please don't stop."

"I won't stop. I promise I won't stop." She slid her hands around to cup his bottom, marveling at the feel of his muscles contracting and relaxing with each powerful thrust.

He slipped his hand between them and began to fondle her, each deft move sending the tension within her coiling tighter. He kissed the soft flesh at the base of her throat. "I want to make it good for you," he murmured. "So good."

She sensed him holding back, waiting for her. When her climax overtook her, he swallowed her cries, then mingled them with his own as his release shuddered through them both.

"I'm glad you stopped fighting this," he said.

"I wasn't fighting," she said.

"You kept pushing me away."

Only because he had such power over her—power to make her forget herself. She didn't trust his motives—or her own.

Chapter Thirteen

Emily woke the next morning with the sun in her eyes and a smile on her face. Last night with Brodie had been better than her best fantasies—and better than she remembered from their younger alliance. There was something to be said for a little maturity when it came to sex.

She had remembered to text Lacy before she went to sleep last night, letting her know she was tucked in safely for the night, in case her friend worried. But she hadn't mentioned she was spending the night with Brodie. For now, she wanted to keep that information to herself. But she supposed she should get back to her own cabin soon, in case someone came looking for her.

She rolled over to face Brodie, who lay asleep on his back, dark stubble emphasizing the strong line of his jaw, his sensuous lips slightly parted. She was just about to lean over and give him a big kiss when pounding on the door shook the cabin. "Brodie, wake up!" a man shouted.

Brodie sat up, instantly alert. "Who is it?" he called.

"It's Travis," Emily whispered, even as her brother identified himself.

"Quick, go in the bathroom." Brodie urged her toward the one interior door in the cabin, then swung his feet to the floor and reached for the jeans he'd discarded last night.

Emily gathered the sheet around her and shuffled to the bathroom, only partially closing the door and positioning herself so that she could see out. Brodie opened the door and Travis—scarily pressed and polished as always—said, "They've found Lynn Wallace's car."

"Where?" Brodie held the door partially closed and stepped back. Emily realized he was attempting to kick the clothing she had left on the floor under the bed.

Travis frowned and tried to move into the cabin, but Brodie blocked the move. "Never mind. You can give me all the details on the way there. Just give me a minute to get dressed."

Brodie tried to shut the door, but Travis pushed past him. "What are you trying to hide?" he asked.

"Nothing, I—" Brodie protested, but Emily had heard enough. She moved out of the bathroom, still clutching the sheet around her.

"Brodie is trying to be a gentleman and hide me," she said. "But there's no need for that. We're all adults here."

Travis's face turned white, then red. "Emily, what do you think you're doing?" he finally snapped out.

As gracefully as she could, she bent and retrieved her clothes from the floor. "I'm going to get dressed so that I can come with you to look at Lynn's car."

"You are not coming with us," Travis said.

"I'm part of the investigative team," she said. "I want to see where the car was left and what kind of condition it's in. That may help me reach some more conclusions about Alex." Plus, she knew how annoyed Travis would be at having her push her way in like this. Her brother was a good man, but he was far too uptight, and she saw it as her duty to force him to loosen up a little.

"We don't need a civilian at a potential crime scene," Travis said.

"You can ride with me, but you have to stay in the vehicle until I clear you to get out," Brodie said.

Travis glared at him, no doubt perturbed at having Brodie overrule him. But Brodie didn't work for Travis, so Emily supposed he could make his own decisions.

"Okay." Clothes in hand, she turned back toward the bathroom.

"It is not okay," Travis said.

"Just give me a minute to get dressed," Brodie said. "I'm sure we can work this out."

Smiling to herself, Emily shut the bathroom door behind her. Later, she was sure she'd have to endure a lecture from her brother about how she was mak-

ing a big mistake getting back together with Brodie.
And maybe he was right. But at least this time she
was going into the relationship with her eyes wide
open. She would have a good time with Brodie now,
and avoid thinking about forever.

TRAVIS INSISTED THE three of them travel together in
his sheriff's department SUV. Brodie reluctantly
agreed. He firmly believed in picking his battles,
and arguing over how they were going to get to a
crime scene wasn't on his list for today. Not with
the promise of a bigger fight looming, judging by
the icy stare Travis kept giving him. Fine. The two
of them could clear the air later, preferably when
Emily wasn't around.

As for the woman in question, Travis's little sister looked smug and satisfied, which should have
felt more gratifying than it did. Brodie wasn't certain if she was so pleased with herself because of the
fantastic sex they had enjoyed the night before—or
because she'd managed to upset her usually unemotional brother.

Dwight met them at the barricade that blocked the
still-closed road. He shifted the orange-and-white
pylons to one side to allow Travis's vehicle to pass,
then walked up to meet them after Travis had parked
behind Dwight's cruiser.

Lynn Wallace's white Volvo sat crookedly across
the northbound lane, both front doors open. "The
crew working to clear the road found it like this when

they reported for work this morning," Dwight said. "They left at about five o'clock yesterday, so someone drove it up here after that."

"Were the doors open like that, or did they open them?" Travis asked.

"They said they were open," Dwight said. "I think whoever dumped it here wanted to make sure it was noticed, and that people saw what was inside."

"What was inside?" Emily asked. She was pale and looked a little frightened, but stood her ground.

"Not another body, thank goodness," Dwight said. "Come take a look."

"Emily, you stay back here," Travis said.

"I won't compromise your crime scene," she said. "I know better than that." Not waiting for an answer, she started toward the car, so that Travis had to hurry to catch up with and pass her.

Brodie followed more slowly, so that by the time he arrived at the car, the others were gathered around, bent over and peering into the open doors. Emily took a step back and motioned for him to move in ahead of her.

The white upholstery of the Volvo, both front and back seats, had been slashed, long diagonal cuts leaving leather hanging in strips, stuffing pulled out and spilling onto the floor. Dull red liquid lay in pools on the seats and dripped onto the floor. "It's paint, not blood," Dwight said. "Regular latex. Most of it is still wet, probably from the cold. I took photos when I arrived, but the snow around the vehicle was pretty churned up. I think all the construction guys probably had a look."

The car's windshield had been smashed, the glass a spiderweb of cracks, green glass pebbles that had broken off from the cracks glittering on the dash.

Brodie rejoined Emily a short distance from the car. She stood with her arms folded across her stomach, staring at the pavement. "Are you okay?" he asked softly.

She nodded, but didn't speak until Travis joined them. "Alex is really angry," she said, looking at her brother. "Enraged. And he's coming apart."

"You think Alex did this?" Travis asked.

"Yes. I'm not an expert, but I think doing this, leaving the car up here like this, where it was sure to be found, he's sending you a message."

"What kind of message?" Brodie asked.

She glanced at him, then back at her brother. "The next woman he goes after, I think it's going to be more violent."

"And he's going to blame law enforcement for the violence," Brodie said. "We're making him do this because we won't leave him alone."

"Yes," Emily said. "I think you're right."

Travis looked back toward the Volvo, the silence stretching between them. Dwight shifted from one foot to the other. The rumble of the road machinery sounded very far away, muffled by distance and the walls of snow.

"Dwight, take Emily back to the ranch, please,"

Travis said. "Brodie and I will wait for the wrecker to tow the car to our garage for processing."

Emily stiffened, and Brodie expected her to argue with her brother, but she apparently saw the sense in not standing out here in the cold with nothing to do. She headed toward Dwight's cruiser, leaving the deputy to follow.

Brodie waited until Dwight had driven away and he and Travis were alone before he spoke. "If you have something to say to me, say it," he said.

Travis took a step toward Brodie, the brim of his hat shading his face, hiding his expression. Brodie braced himself for a dressing-down. Travis would tell him he had no business sleeping with Emily, that he was here to do a job and not to seduce his sister, that he had used their friendship to take advantage of Emily—nothing Brodie hadn't already told himself or heard before, five years ago, when he and Travis had also argued about Brodie's relationship with Emily. He would let Travis get out all his words and not try to defend himself. Once Travis had exhausted his anger, maybe they could have a civil discussion about Emily and Brodie's feelings for her.

But Travis didn't say anything. He reared back and belted Brodie in the chin, sending him staggering.

Brodie let out a yelp of surprise and managed to stay upright. He rubbed his aching jaw and stared at the sheriff, who was flushed and breathing hard, hands at his sides, still balled into fists. "I reckon you think I deserve that," Brodie said.

"You don't think you do?"

"I had a long talk with your sister last night—before we went to bed together. She told me about the baby." He paused, gathering his emotions. The reality that Emily had been pregnant with his baby—that he could have been a father—was only just beginning to sink in. "I never knew, I swear. She said she wrote to me, but I never got the letter. If I had, you wouldn't have been able to keep me away from her."

Travis glared at him, wary.

"You know I asked her to marry me, right?" Brodie said.

Travis nodded.

"And she turned me down. I didn't dump her—she dumped me. But I would have come back to help her with the baby—in whatever way she wanted me to help."

He could tell the minute the fight went out of Travis. The sheriff's shoulders sagged and he bowed his head. "I'm sorry I let my temper get the best of me," he said.

Brodie rubbed his jaw again. "Maybe it was good for both of us." He offered his hand.

Travis stared at Brodie's hand. "Maybe it's none of my business, but what happens with you and Emily now?" he asked.

"I don't know. A lot of that is up to her. But it's

not going to be a repeat of last time, I promise. Is that good enough for you?"

Travis grasped his hand, then pulled him close and thumped him on the back. "You and Emily are adults, so what you do is your business," he said. He pulled away and his eyes met Brodie's—hard eyes full of meaning. "But if you hurt her again, I promise, I will hunt you down."

Brodie had no doubt of the truth behind those words. "You don't have to worry," he said. "Now come on. The killer is the only man you need to worry about hunting down right now."

"Your fiancé ate my prosciutto."

Saturday afternoon, Emily and Lacy looked up from the place cards they were hand-lettering for that night's wedding rehearsal dinner. The caterer, Bette, stood before them, hands on her hips and a stormy expression in her eyes. "How do you know Travis ate it?" Lacy asked.

"Because I caught him finishing off the last of it before he headed out the door this morning."

Lacy set aside the stack of place cards. "The poor man has been working so much, eating at odd hours. I hope you didn't fuss at him too much."

"I didn't. But I need that prosciutto for the dinner tonight."

"If you think the grocery in Eagle Mountain will have it, I can run and get it for you," Emily said. "I need to go to the office supply store, anyway."

"They don't have it," Bette said. "But Iris at the Cake Walk said she had some she would sell me. If you could fetch it for me, that would be a big help. I have too much to do to get ready for tonight to leave."

"Of course I'll get it." Emily looked at the place cards spread out in front of her. "Lacy and I are almost finished here."

"Don't go to town by yourself," Lacy said. "Find one of the ranch hands to go with you."

"All right." Emily wanted to protest that she would be fine on her own, but the other women Alex had killed would have probably said the same thing. And the possibility that the *EW* on Alex's list might mean her made her even more cautious.

She and Lacy finished the place cards, each hand-lettered, with a tiny silk rose glued to the corner. "They turned out really nice," Emily said as she passed the last of the cards over to Lacy.

"They did." Lacy sighed. For a bride on the eve of her wedding day, she didn't look very happy.

"What's wrong?" Emily asked.

Lacy looked up, her eyes shiny with tears. "I'm being silly. I mean, women have died, and here I am, worrying about my wedding. It's ridiculous." She pressed her fingers to her eyes, blotting the tears.

"You're not being silly." Emily squeezed Lacy's hand. "The wedding is going to be beautiful. By tomorrow afternoon, you'll be married and it will be beautiful."

"I'm so worried something is going to happen to

mess things up," she said. "Not just the wedding, but Travis—this killer hates him." She sniffed. "I know he has a dangerous job, and I told myself I could handle that, but when I think about something happening to him…" She pressed her lips together and looked away.

"Travis is smart and careful, and he loves you so much," Emily said. "Nothing is going to happen to him." She said a silent prayer that this would be true.

Lacy nodded and stood. "You're right. And my worrying won't accomplish anything." She gathered the place cards into a neat pile. "Thanks for your help with these. I think I'll go see if Bette needs me to do anything in the kitchen."

Emily wished she had had more to offer her friend than words. If only she could figure out where Alex was hiding. Finding and arresting him would allow Travis and Lacy to start their marriage off right, with a honeymoon away from all this stress and no lingering worries about local women dying.

She gathered her purse, slipped on her coat and went in search of someone to accompany her to town. She searched the barns and outbuildings, and stopped to check on Witchy, who was contentedly munching hay, her leg showing no signs of further inflammation. No one was at the bunkhouse or in the machine shed. Maybe the men had decided to make themselves scarce while the last frantic preparations for tomorrow's wedding were being completed.

On her way back from the barn she walked past

the row of guest cabins. The door to Brodie's cabin opened and he stepped out onto the porch. Odd that he'd be here this time of day. "Brodie!" she called.

He turned to face her and she winced. The left side of his jaw was red and swollen. "What happened to you?" she asked, hurrying up the steps to him.

He gingerly touched his jaw. "I put ice on it, hoping to get the swelling down."

"What happened?" When she had left him and Travis on Dixon Pass, they had been waiting for the wrecker to arrive.

"It's no big deal." He took her arm and urged her down the steps alongside him. "By tomorrow you won't even know it happened."

"You're not answering my question." She studied the injury more closely. She was no expert, but she was pretty sure someone had punched him. "Who hit you?"

"You don't want to know."

Had he tried to arrest someone and they fought back? No, he wouldn't bother hiding that information from her. In fact, she could think of only one person he might try to shield. "Did *Travis* punch you?" The last word came out as a squeak—she couldn't quite hold back her shock at the idea. Travis was so even-tempered. So aggravatingly calm almost all of the time.

But he definitely hadn't been pleased to find her and Brodie together this morning.

"It's no big deal," Brodie said again.

"Did you hit him back?" She clutched at his arm. "Lacy is going to be furious if you broke Travis's nose or something on the eve of the wedding."

"No, I didn't hit him back." He stopped walking and turned to face her. "I figured he needed the one punch to let off some of the pressure that's been building up with this case."

"Then he should go split wood or something— not punch you."

"Don't worry about it," he said. "We cleared the air, and everything is okay now."

"What did you tell him?"

He caressed her shoulders and spoke more softly. "I told him I never got your letter about the baby— that if I had, I never would have left you to deal with that alone. I still hate that you had to go through that by yourself."

The pain in his voice brought a lump to her throat. She moved in closer and his arms went around her. They couldn't do anything to change the past, but at least now she knew he really hadn't deserted her when she needed him most. She wondered what would have happened if he had received her letter and come back to her. Would they have married, anyway? She knew she'd been right to turn down his proposal, but would knowing a child was on the way have changed her mind? She closed her eyes and pushed the thought away. The answer to that question didn't matter now.

Brodie patted her back. "What are you thinking?" he asked.

"Travis still shouldn't have hit you," she mumbled against his chest.

"It's okay," he said. "It was something we both needed, I think."

She raised her head to look at him. "Men are weird."

He laughed. "Now that that's settled, what are you up to?"

"I promised Bette I'd run to town and pick up some prosciutto for her. I was looking for someone to go with me. Want to volunteer?"

"Absolutely. What is Bette doing with prosciutto?"

"Something wonderful, I'm sure. It's for the rehearsal dinner tonight."

"I'd almost forgotten there's a wedding tomorrow."

"How could you forget? There's a big silver-and-white wreath on every door in the house—and the door of your cabin. Not to mention the wedding gifts in the hall and everyone running around like crazy people trying to get ready."

"I said almost. Besides, I've been focused on other things."

Right. Everything always came back to the killer. Alex would probably be thrilled to know how much he was directing all their lives. She couldn't even go to the store by herself because of him. "Come on," she said. "Let's go. I have a million things to do before the dinner tonight."

On the way into town they didn't discuss Alex, or the wedding, or even the weather—all topics Emily felt had been exhausted in recent weeks. Instead, they talked about their lives on the other side of Colorado—she in Fort Collins and he in Denver. "In the spring there's a great farmers market every weekend," she told him. "I go sometimes just to hang out and people watch."

"Do you ever go hiking out around Horsetooth Falls?" he asked.

"It's been a while, but it's a great area."

"We should hike it together sometime," he said.

Her heart gave a funny little flutter. "Yeah. Yeah, we should."

He parked at the curb in front of the Cake Walk Café and followed Emily inside. The lunch crowd had dissipated, but people sat at a couple of tables, nursing cups of coffee or polishing off the last of a meal. The café's owner, Iris Desmet, waved from behind a counter at the back of the room. She disappeared into the kitchen and emerged a moment later with a paper-wrapped parcel. "I warned Bette that I've had this in my freezer for a while," she said as she punched keys on the cash register. "But she said she was desperate, so I told her she could have it for a discount."

"I'm sure it will be fine," Emily said. "Will we see you at the wedding tomorrow?"

"Of course. There's nothing like a wedding to cheer people up, and we could certainly use a little of that—though I hear the road may open tomorrow, and the weather forecast doesn't show any more snow for a couple of weeks. Maybe the rest of the winter won't be as hard."

"I hope that's true." Emily handed over her credit card and waited while Iris swiped it, then she signed the receipt and tucked the package of prosciutto into her purse.

On the sidewalk, Dwight hailed them from across the street. "I thought you'd want to know what we found in the car once we started going through it," he said.

"Let me guess," Brodie said. "One of the Ice Cold calling cards."

Dwight nodded. "Better than that—we found some good prints in the paint. They match ones on file for Alex Woodruff."

"I don't think we had any doubt who was responsible, but it's nice to have more evidence," Brodie said.

"When you get a chance, we've got a couple of questions for the CBI profiler."

Emily put a hand on Brodie's back to get his attention. "You two talk shop. I'm going to the office supply store to pick up a few things."

Brodie frowned. "I'll only be a minute."

"And the store is only two doors down." She

pointed to the building with the oversize gold paperclip over the door. "You can see it from here."

He nodded, then turned back to Dwight. Smiling to herself, she hurried toward the office supply. She couldn't say why she was so happy—there was still a killer on the loose, the highway leading out of town was still closed and everyone around her was keyed up over the wedding tomorrow. And it wasn't as if she and Brodie had resolved anything. She felt closer to him now, and they'd had a night of great sex. Maybe after this was all over, they'd get together again to hike or, who knows, maybe even go out on a real date. That was still no reason for the almost giddy lightness that made her want to skip down the sidewalk and had her fighting back a goofy smile.

The bells on the door of the Paperclip jangled as she entered. The owner, Eleanor Davis, who had taught Emily when she was in third grade, waved from in front of a display of earbuds and went back to assisting an older gentleman. Emily wandered down the aisles of office supplies, admiring a beautiful pen here or an attractive notebook there. She could have spent hours in here, running her hands over the displays and breathing in the scents of ink and paper, but settled for choosing a package of colorful note cards, a sturdy wire-bound journal and a purple gel ink pen. What could she say—some women experienced euphoria when buying new shoes, while office supplies did it for her.

Outside on the sidewalk, she almost collided with

an elderly man. "So sorry, miss," he said, holding out
his hands defensively. He stared out at her from behind thick glasses, his expression confused and his
eyes bloodshot. His gray hair hung lank to his shoulders and a wisp of a gray beard stood out against sal-
low skin and sagging jowls. "Clumsy of me, I..." He
looked around, blinking. "I think I need some help."

The poor dear looked really out of it. Emily glanced
across the street, hoping to see Dwight and Brodie and
wave them over, but they must have gone back into
the café—probably to get out of the biting wind. She
shifted her purchases to one hand. "What can I do to
help you?" she asked.

"It's my car. There's something wrong with it."

"Let me call someone for you." She fumbled in
her purse for her phone.

"No." He put out a hand to stop her. "Don't go to
so much trouble. I know what's wrong. I just need
to find the auto parts store."

"There's one out on the highway," she said. "Near
the motel. But it's a little far to walk in this weather."

"You could give me a ride," he said. "I know it's
a lot to ask, but it would help me so much."

She glanced toward the café again. "I'm with
someone," she said. "But I'm sure he wouldn't mind
giving you a ride—"

"No!" The man's hand clamped around her
wrist—hard. Startled, she stared at him. The confused look had vanished from his eyes, and he no

longer looked so old. Something sharp pricked her side—a knife. "Come with me now, and don't make a scene," he said.

Chapter Fourteen

Emily opened her mouth to scream, but no sound emerged. The old man put his arm around her, pulling her close. The odors of wood smoke and sweat stung her nose, and the knife dug into her side, so that it hurt to even breathe deeply. She dropped her purse, the contents spilling out onto the sidewalk, the package of ham coming to rest in a snowbank. "That's right, come along nice and easy," the man— she was sure it was Alex—crooned.

He still looked like an innocent old man, but nothing about him was harmless. He had a grip like iron—she imagined him breaking her wrist if she tried to jerk away. And then he would slash her open with the knife before she had time to run.

"Hey!" The shout boomed out, making her jump. Alex turned, dragging her around with him, and she stared as Brodie raced toward them. She had the sensation of being somewhere outside herself, watching a slow-motion movie—Alex opening his mouth to say something, Brodie reaching into his coat and pulling out a gun—the knife pressing harder against her side.

Then everything sped up. Someone screamed, Brodie shouted, then Alex shoved her away, so hard that she fell, slamming her knees into the concrete of the walkway. Brodie's boots thundered past her, then a woman knelt beside her, trying to help her to her feet.

But Emily didn't get up until Brodie returned. He bent over her, chest heaving, the gun out of sight now. For a long moment, neither of them said a thing, their eyes locked, his expression reflecting all the terror she felt. "Are you…all right?" he managed to gasp at last.

She nodded, though she still couldn't seem to speak. By now a crowd had gathered, everyone wanting to know what had happened, and if they could help. Brodie grasped Emily's hand and pulled her to her feet. She caught her breath at the sudden sharp pain in her side, and clamped her hand over the spot. "He had a knife," she said.

Brodie pushed her hand away, then yanked down the zipper of her coat and shoved it aside. She stared at the quarter-sized blossom of red against the white of her sweater. "We need to get you to the clinic," he said, then, without waiting for a reply, scooped her into his arms and started across the street.

"Brodie, put me down. Please!" She beat her fists against his chest, but his expression never changed. People called after them, a car braked to a halt as he stepped in front of it and horns honked, but Brodie appeared to hear none of it. He burst into the Eagle Mountain medical clinic and everyone in the small waiting room stared at them.

"She's hurt," he said. "She needs to see the doctor now."

She wanted to demand once more that he put her down, but doubted he would even hear her. When the door leading to the examination rooms opened, he carried her through it and into the closest empty room. A woman with a stethoscope followed them inside. "What is the meaning—"

But she got no further. Brodie took out his badge and shoved it at her, then pulled back Emily's coat to show the spot of blood. "She's been stabbed."

The woman's eyes widened, but she recovered quickly and took charge. She pushed Brodie out of the way, then eased the coat off Emily and pulled up the sweater.

In the end, Emily needed four stitches, a tetanus shot and some antibiotics to ward off infection. Brodie sat in a chair, scowling and silent, while the nurse practitioner on duty stitched up Emily. No one talked about what had happened, and Emily didn't know if she was relieved about that or not.

The nurse had just finished administering the tetanus vaccine when someone knocked on the door. "It's the sheriff," Travis said. "May I come in?"

"You might as well," the nurse practitioner said, and shifted so that Travis could squeeze in behind her.

"I'm fine," Emily said, sliding off the exam table, wincing a little at the pain in her side. "It was just a little cut."

Travis's answer was to pull her close and squeeze her so tight she couldn't breathe. Her brother wasn't much for words, but the concern in that hug made her tear up, and she had to force herself to smile and push him away. "I'm okay," she said. "Really."

Brodie stood and Travis turned to him. "I've got everyone available out looking for this guy, but I'm afraid he's done another disappearing act."

"Let's talk about this outside," Brodie said. He picked up Emily's coat and helped her back into it. Then, one hand on her back, he followed her into the waiting room, where, once again, everyone stared at them.

"Someone brought these for you," the receptionist said, and handed over Emily's purse, the package of office supplies and the paper-wrapped parcel of prosciutto. Emily stared at the ham, teary again. It felt like hours since she had set out to run a simple errand for Bette, yet the prosciutto was still cold.

"Let's go to my office," Travis said, and escorted them out of the clinic. The three of them piled into his cruiser, Brodie in the back seat with her. She lay her head on his shoulder, closed her eyes and tried not to think about what had happened, although she knew she would have to give a statement to Travis. All she wanted was a few more minutes to pretend she hadn't just come within seconds of death.

At the station, Adelaide clucked over her and brought her a cup of tea. "Drink that," she ordered. "And don't let these two bully you into anything." She scowled at Brodie and Travis as if she blamed them for the attack, then left, closing the door to Travis's office behind her with a solid *Click!*

"I'm not going to bully you," Travis said. "But we need to know what happened. We got a description of the man who attacked you from a few people, but about all they said was that it was an old guy with a patchy beard, and none of them remembered seeing him before."

She took a long sip of the sweet, hot tea, then set the cup on the edge of the desk and took a deep breath. She could do this. She was alive and safe and what she had to say might help Travis and Brodie stop this man. "It was Alex," she said. "I didn't recognize him because he was wearing a disguise. A good one. But I'm sure it was him."

"Start with a description," Travis said. "We'll go from there."

She described the old man who had approached her—his glasses and long hair and saggy jowls. "He looked confused and harmless," she said. "Stooped over and a little shaky. I felt sorry for him. He wanted me to feel sorry for him, to not see him as a threat. I'm sure that's what he did with the other women, too."

"He didn't run like an old man," Brodie said. "He

took off like a track star. He ducked down an alley and I lost him within seconds."

"He said he was having car trouble and asked me for a ride to the auto parts store," Emily said. "When I told him I was with someone, and started toward the café, he grabbed my wrist and stuck the knife in my side. His whole demeanor changed. That's when I knew it was Alex." She swallowed hard, remembered terror making her light-headed.

"I came out of the café with Dwight and saw Emily cozied up with this old guy," Brodie said. "Even though her back was to me, something about the situation didn't look right. When I called to them, the guy swung her around toward me. He looked angry—enraged—and I could see that Emily was terrified. I drew my weapon and ordered him to stop. At first I thought he would resist, or try to use Emily as a shield. Instead, he released her and took off running." He raked a hand through his hair. "I should have insisted you stay with me. And I never should have gone into the café with Dwight."

"I was in a public place with other people all around," Emily said. "What was Alex thinking?"

"He thinks he's invincible," Travis said. "That law enforcement is stupid and we'll never catch him. But we will."

A knock on the door interrupted them. "Come in," Travis called.

Dwight entered, a bundle of cloth in his hand.

"We found these in the trash bins behind Mo's Pub," he said, and laid the bundle on the desk.

Emily stared at the drab shirt, thick glasses with scratched lenses, and thin gray beard and long hair. "That was his disguise," she said.

"I figure he ditched the clothes and either put on another disguise or walked away as himself," Dwight said.

"He's good at blending in," Emily said. "He can be noticed when he wants to be, but when he doesn't, he fades into the crowd."

"I interviewed some of his professors over the phone," Travis said. "Most of them didn't even remember him."

"He's decided to go after you now," Brodie said.

"But why? Because I knew him at school?"

"Maybe," Brodie said. "Or because you're Travis's sister. He wants to prove he's better than any cop."

She welcomed the anger that surged through her at the thought. It made her feel stronger. She stood. "I'm not going to sit quietly and play victim for his sick fantasies."

"No, you're not," Brodie agreed. "And he's not going to get close enough to hurt you again." He stood also, and took her hand in his. "Because from now on, I'm not letting you out of my sight."

THAT EVENING, BRODIE sat in the Walkers' living room as Emily descended the stairs to the strains of Pachelbel's Canon. Something tugged hard at his chest as she paused at the bottom of the stairs and met his gaze, then she ducked her head and turned away to take her place in front of the fire, where the officiant, a plump woman with auburn hair, waited for the run-through of the wedding ceremony.

The other bridesmaids followed—Gage's wife, Maya, Paige Riddell and Brenda Prentice. The music switched to the traditional bridal entrance tune and Lacy, in a blue lace dress, carrying an imaginary bouquet, appeared at the top of the stairs. Even though this was only a rehearsal, Brodie and the other observers rose as Lacy descended the stairs.

Rather than watch the bride, Brodie kept his eyes on Travis, who stood with Gage, Ryder Stewart, Nate Harris and Cody Rankin in the archway between the living and dining room. The sheriff's stance was casual: hip cocked, face impassive. But as Lacy neared, Travis straightened, then reached out his hand to her. In that moment, Brodie was sure Travis wasn't thinking about a killer or the women who had died, or about anything but this woman and their future together.

Love had the power to do that—to push aside every worry and distraction, to focus attention on what mattered most, on life and hope, even in the midst of tragedy.

Brodie shifted his gaze to Emily. She was watching her brother and Lacy, eyes shiny with unshed tears, joy radiating from her smile. Brodie's heart hammered and he had trouble catching his breath, the knowledge of how much he loved her a sucker punch to the gut.

If only she would look at him, and let him see that she felt the same—that she loved him. But her eyes remained fixed on the bride and groom as the officiant explained what would happen next.

"You may practice kissing the bride if you like," the officiant said. Everyone laughed as Travis moved in to kiss Lacy and the spell was broken.

"Now that that's over, we can eat," Gage said, ignoring the scolding look from Maya.

Brodie stood and went to Emily. Though he was not a member of the wedding party, and had not even received an invitation to the wedding, Travis had embraced the idea of Brodie as Emily's bodyguard. He had also apparently persuaded his mother and father that Brodie was not the scoundrel they had assumed and now they, too, seemed happy to have him protecting their daughter.

As for Emily, he wasn't certain what she felt about him becoming, by default, her "plus-one" for the wedding. She smiled as he held her chair for her, next to his at the table, then quickly turned her attention to the other guests. Most of the wedding party was made up of other law enforcement officers and their spouses or significant others.

Travis and the bride-to-be sat side by side in the middle of the long table, Lacy smiling and beautiful, Travis stoic and tense, his smiles doled out sparingly for his beloved. He was putting on a good show, but

Brodie knew his mind was back on Alex. Like Brodie, he was probably wondering if, while they ate and drank and toasted the happy couple, the Ice Cold Killer was claiming another victim.

The officiant, Reverend Winger, sat across the table. As Bette and the ranch cook, Rainey, set salads in front of the guests, she leaned across and asked, "Are you in law enforcement, too?"

"Yes, ma'am. I'm a detective with the Colorado Bureau of Investigation."

"This must be the safest place to be in the whole county right now," Reverend Winger said.

"Reverend Winger, I understand you vacationed in Italy last year." Lacy leaned across to address the pastor. "What was your favorite thing about that trip?"

As the reverend launched into a description of her visit to Tuscany, Brodie silently applauded Lacy. Before the rehearsal began, she had laid down the law—absolutely no discussion of the case tonight. *We're going to focus on the wedding and be happy*, she had insisted.

"The prosciutto doesn't look any worse for wear," Emily leaned over and whispered to Brodie as a plate of prosciutto-wrapped asparagus and petite sirloin steaks was set before each of them.

"No one will ever know," he said, and popped a bite of the asparagus into his mouth. No one would know what Emily had been through earlier that day, either. If he detected a little more tension around her eyes, that was only because he was so focused on her.

"You know, it's hard to eat when you're staring at me like that," she said.

"Sorry." He was tempted to say something about her being so beautiful he couldn't keep his eyes off her, but he was sure such a cheesy line would only make her groan. He focused on his own food. "This is delicious," he said. "Bette did a great job."

"She really did," Emily agreed. "Though in addition to the stress of my prosciutto problem, she had to deal with a no-show by the florist." She gestured toward the center of the table, where an arrangement of greens and pine cones, tied with silver ribbon, filled a silver vase. "This was a last-minute substitution."

"What did the florist have to say about the failed delivery?" he asked.

"By the time Bette had a chance to call, they were already closed. But she left a stern message—and she's going to double-check with them in the morning to make sure the wedding flowers get here in time."

"I'll be sure and tell her everything looks—and tastes—great."

"Speech! Speech!" Nate Harris, at one end of the table, tapped his spoon against his water glass.

Travis's father shoved back his chair and stood as the guests fell quiet. "Thank you, everyone, for coming here this evening," he said. "I especially want to thank Bette and Rainey for putting on such a lovely dinner."

Cries of "hear, hear" and light applause followed this remark.

Mr. Walker turned to Travis and Lacy. "Your mother and I have looked forward to tomorrow for a long time," he said. "We're so happy to welcome Lacy into the family and we wish you only the best." He raised his glass in a toast and everyone followed suit.

"Is this where everyone else in the wedding party feels compelled to also give a toast?" Emily whispered to Brodie. "If it is, I'm going to need more wine."

But instead of toasts, Bette arrived with dessert— a baked Alaska that Brodie, at least, would have awarded first place in any bake-off.

Half an hour later, stuffed and happy, the guests who weren't staying on the ranch made their way to the door. Brodie stood with Emily, saying goodbye. When everyone was gone, Brodie led Emily aside, where they could talk without being overheard. "About the arrangements for tonight," he said. "I meant what I said before about not letting you out of my sight."

"So you're saying we have to sleep together?" He couldn't decide if the look in her eye was teasing or not.

"I'm saying I'm going to spend the night in the same room as you—sex is optional."

"Alex isn't going to come into this house and up to my bedroom," she said. "He wouldn't dare!"

"I wouldn't put anything past him at this point." After all, Alex had tried to crash the barbecue Wednesday night. Brodie took her arm and pulled her closer. "I'm not going to give him any opportunity to get to you again." The memory of her crumpled on the sidewalk, bleeding from Alex's knife, still made it hard to breathe.

"All right." Her smile made the tight band around his chest ease. "I was planning on sneaking out to your cabin later, anyway." She snuggled against him.

"Oh, you were?" He lowered his head to kiss her, but an uproar at the front door made them pull apart and turn toward the clamor. Lacy's parents, who had been among the first to leave, stood with Travis and Lacy—Mrs. Milligan in tears, her husband white-faced. "That poor woman," Mrs. Milligan moaned.

Brodie moved toward them, Emily close behind, as Dwight shoved through the crowd. "The florist van is blocking the end of the driveway," he said. "The delivery driver is inside, dead."

Chapter Fifteen

Emily urged Brodie to go with Travis and the others to investigate the crime scene, but he insisted on staying by her side as she helped her mother and Lacy soothe the Milligans. She volunteered to let Lacy's parents stay in her room that evening. Her own parents didn't ask where she planned to spend the night, though she was aware of her mother watching her and Brodie more closely as the evening progressed.

Several hours passed before the other guests could leave. While they waited for the crime scene investigators and coroner to finish their work, for the ambulance to remove the body and for the wrecker to arrive to tow the van to the sheriff's garage, Emily poured coffee and served snacks that no one ate, and tried to make small talk about anything but the murders.

It was after midnight before she was able to retrieve her clothes and toiletries, along with a change of clothes for the next day, from her room and go with Brodie to his cabin. She should have been exhausted by the strain of the day, but instead felt hyperalert and on edge. Halfway down the path to the cabins, she put her arm out to stop Brodie. "Stop just a minute," she said. "This feels like the first time things have been quiet all day and I want to take it in."

She closed her eyes and breathed in deeply of the cold, clear air, then tilted her head back and stared up at the night sky, thousands of stars glittering against the velvet blackness.

"It's beautiful," Brodie said, standing behind her and wrapping his arms around her.

"It's surreal to think of violence in the midst of such peace," she said. "Especially while we were celebrating such a happy occasion."

He kissed the top of her head—such a sweet, gentle gesture. "Come on," he said. "You're shivering. It's warm in the cabin."

The cabin was warm and neat, the bed made and clutter put away. Was this because Brodie had been expecting her to stay with him tonight, or because he was a neat and organized guy? She suspected a little of both. "I want to change out of this dress and these heels," she said, staring down at her fashionable, but definitely chilly, attire.

"Go right ahead," Brodie said.

She retreated to the bathroom, where she changed into yoga pants and a T-shirt. She studied her reflection in the mirror over the sink, hesitating, then fusing responses to Brodie reduce her to a sodden puddle of feelings.

The wedding was scheduled to take place at five o'clock. Before then, there was still a lot to do to prepare for the ceremony. Bette appeared in the doorway to the dining room as Emily and Brodie were finishing up breakfast. "I need you two to help with the decorations," she said.

"Sure." Emily handed her dirty dishes to Brodie, who had volunteered to carry them into the kitchen. "What can we do?"

"Give me those." Bette took the dishes, then dumped them in a bus tub on the end of the sideboard. "Needless to say, things are as chaotic at the florist's this morning as they are here, and we may not be getting all the flowers we ordered, so we're making some last-minute adjustments. Come with me."

She led them through the living room, where she had assembled a pile of evergreens, silver ribbon and a mass of white silk flowers. "I raided the attic and the rest of the house for every flower arrangement on the premises," Bette explained. "Now we're going to use them to transform this room into a woodland winter wonderland."

Under Bette's direction, Emily and Brodie began cutting and wiring the greenery to make garland. Bette came along behind them and attached ribbons and flowers. "I guess the florist was pretty upset

turned on the water and washed off her makeup, then brushed out her hair. It wasn't as if Brodie hadn't seen her like this before.

"How is your side doing?" he asked when she emerged from the bathroom. He had removed his shoes and untucked his shirt, and his gun lay on the table beside the bed.

She made a face. "It hurts some," she said. She had been mostly successful at distracting herself from the pain. "It's more annoying than anything."

"Do you mind if I have a look?" he asked.

"All right."

He crossed the room to her and carefully lifted up the T. When she had changed for dinner earlier, she had removed the dressing, so that the stitches were exposed, the skin slightly puffy around the neat row of dark thread. Brodie studied the wound for a moment, then bent and gently kissed the skin above the stitches.

She threaded her fingers through his hair and held him to her for a moment, before dragging his face up to hers and kissing him. She molded her body to his, enjoying the feel of him so close, the anticipation of spending another night getting to know him even better like a pleasant hum through her.

"I don't want to hurt you," he murmured, his mouth against her hair.

"You won't." Not physically, at least. She wouldn't think about what might happen if he left her again.

They kissed again, heat building, and were moving toward the bed when someone knocked on the door. Brodie turned toward the sound. "It's Travis. Can I come in?"

Brodie opened the door and Travis entered. He looked cold and exhausted, Emily thought. He needed a hot drink and a good night's sleep, but she doubted he would get either. He glanced at Emily, then turned to Brodie. "I wanted to update you on what we found," he said.

"Emily will have to stay and hear." Brodie sat on the side of the bed and Emily settled next to him.

"All right." Travis took the chair and sat with his elbows on his knees, head down. "The woman is Sarah Geraldi, a part-time delivery person for the florist," he said. "She was killed like the others, hands and feet bound, the Ice Cold calling card tucked into her bra." He glanced at Emily again. "You were right. There was more violence this time. He cut her up pretty badly, and there was more blood."

"He would probably have blood on him," Brodie said. "He's not being as careful."

"He knows you know who he is," Emily said. "He's not trying to hide his identity anymore. In fact, I think he likes knowing you know that he's the one who's getting the better of you. At least, I think that's how he sees it."

Travis nodded. "The medical examiner thinks she was killed much earlier today, hidden in the van, then driven here a short time ago. The delivery van's engine was still warm."

"He killed her someplace else and brough[t] here to taunt you," Brodie said.

Travis nodded. "It looks that way."

"If Alex drove the van here with the body in[side,] how did he get away?" Brodie asked. "Has he re[?]cruited another accomplice? Stashed another vehicl[e] somewhere? It's still seven miles to town."

"Maybe he didn't leave." Travis raised his head, his gaze steady, his expression grim. "Maybe he's still here, hiding somewhere."

TRAVIS'S ANNOUNCEMENT DID nothing to help Emily or Brodie sleep. They made love tenderly, but with an air of desperation, eager to suppress, at least for a little while, thoughts of the horror that might lurk outside the door. They both woke early and dressed without saying much, then made their way up the path to the house. Brodie walked with one arm around Emily, the other hand on his gun, constantly scanning around them for any sign of an intruder.

"I'm jumpy enough without you acting as if Alex is going to leap out of the bushes and grab me," she said. "You heard Travis—he had every extra man searching around here last night. Alex isn't here."

"I don't believe in taking chances when the stakes are so high," Brodie said.

The look he gave her had a lot of heat behind it, and she had to look away. She really needed to keep her emotions in check so that she could sup[port] Lacy today. She couldn't afford to let her o[wn]

when she got the news about her employee," Emily said as she snipped a section of pine branches.

"It's even worse than you think," Bette said. "The woman who was murdered was the shop owner's daughter."

"Oh, no!" Emily's chest tightened in sympathy for the poor woman.

"Believe me, I'd gladly throttle Alex Woodruff with my bare hands if I could find him." Bette yanked hard on the end of a silver bow. "Not only am I sick over all the women he's killed, but I hate that this has cast such a pall over the wedding. Lacy, of all people, deserves to be happy on this day."

"Of course she does," Emily murmured in sympathy. Travis deserved to be happy, too—and he wouldn't be until Alex was arrested and locked behind bars, where he couldn't hurt anyone else.

"Oh, Bette, it's going to look wonderful."

The three of them turned to see Lacy, dressed in black yoga pants and a too-large sweatshirt that had *Rayford County Sheriff's Dept.* emblazoned across the front, her hair rolled up in large foam rollers, her face pale from both lack of makeup and lack of sleep, and her eyes dull with a frazzled, distracted expression. She moved into the room and fingered a white silk rose, and a single tear rolled down her cheek.

"Oh, honey, it's going to be all right." Bette enfolded her friend in a hug.

Lacy gave in and sobbed on Bette's shoulder. "This is supposed to be the happiest day of my life," she said between tears. "And I'm so worried and scared and angry. What if something happens to Travis? What if someone else gets hurt? It's just so awful." And a fresh wave of weeping engulfed her.

Bette patted her back and looked over her shoulder at Emily and Brodie. "You two can finish up here, can't you?" she asked. "The garland is mostly done—you just need to add a few more bows and then put it around the archway." She indicated the arch between the living and dining room, where Lacy and Travis would stand to recite their vows.

"Of course we can," Emily said.

Bette nodded. "Come on, Lacy, let's go fix you a cup of tea and get something to take the puffiness out of your eyes," she said, leading the distraught bride away. "Everything is going to be fine."

Emily and Brodie finished the garland. Emily didn't think her bows looked as professional as Bette's, but she told herself everyone was going to be focused on the happy couple, and not the decorations. "You'll have to start attaching this over the archway," she said, handing Brodie a length of garland. "I'm not tall enough to do it without a ladder."

"What do I attach it with?" he asked.

She searched the table and spotted a staple gun. "Use this." She handed it to him. "If Mom complains later, I'll take the blame."

He positioned the garland, pressed the staple gun against it and…*click!* He frowned. "I think it's out of staples."

"I know where they are," she said, and raced to retrieve the box. Her mother kept all her household tools in an old pie safe at one end of the front porch. She hurried to the cabinet and found the box, half full of staples, and let out a sigh of relief. One less thing to worry about.

She was halfway back to the front door when a plaintive cry stopped her. She held her breath, listening, and it came again. "Tawny?" she called, and the cat answered, sounding even more distressed than before. She must have decided to have her kittens near the house, but where?

Emily moved to the end of the porch. "Tawny?"

The cry came again. Was the cat under one of the cars? Was she hurt? Heart hammering, Emily hurried toward the sounds of distress. "Tawny!" she called again, and bent to look underneath Brodie's SUV.

Strong arms grabbed her from behind, and a hand slapped over her mouth so that she couldn't cry out, and she couldn't move. She stared up into Alex's face. "Isn't this going to be a nice surprise for the sheriff on his wedding day?" he asked.

Chapter Sixteen

Brodie was about to go after Emily when Bette called to him from the other room. "Brodie, can you come in here a minute, please?"

He looked after Emily, who was closing the front door behind her.

"Lacy wants to speak to you," Bette said.

Telling himself Emily would be fine, he followed the sound of Bette's voice to the sunporch, where she and Lacy sat with teacups in hand. Lacy beckoned him. "I have a favor to ask," she said, and patted the love seat beside her.

"Of course." He perched on the edge of the seat, anxious to get this over with so he could check on Emily.

"Promise me you'll see that Travis gets to the altar for the wedding," she said. "There are plenty of other law enforcement officers here today who can handle things for a while. All I need are a couple of hours of Travis's undivided attention so that we can get married."

He nodded. "Of course." Though the sheriff was in charge of the case, there was no reason he couldn't take a break for a few hours.

"I'm going to find Gage and make him promise the same thing," Lacy said. "And any of the other officers who are here today." She set her teacup aside and stood. "And now I'd better get upstairs and take my bath. Paige is coming by soon to do my nails."

"I've got plenty to do, too," Bette said, standing also. "Brodie, did you and Emily finish the decorations?"

"Emily went to get more staples. I'll go find her." She had been gone much too long, he thought, quickening his pace through the house.

He grabbed his jacket from the hooks by the door and pulled it on as he stepped out onto the porch. The door to a cabinet at the end of the porch stood open. The cabinet contained a hammer and other small tools, paintbrushes, some flowerpots and other items that might be useful for minor repairs or outdoor decorating. Was this where Emily had retrieved the staples? But where was she?

A gray tabby cat came around the side of the house, heavily pregnant belly swaying from side to side. She jumped up onto the porch and rubbed herself against his legs. Brodie ignored her and stepped off the porch, studying the snow. Footprints overlaid each other in the snow on the edges of the shoveled path, but none stood out as particularly fresh, and he couldn't tell if any of them were Emily's.

A sheriff's department SUV pulled up in front of the house and Travis climbed out. "Are you hiding out here from the wedding chaos?" Travis asked.

Brodie opened his mouth to share his concern about Emily, then closed it again, remembering his promise to Lacy. Travis needed to focus on the wedding today. If Brodie needed help, there were plenty of other people around here who were qualified to give it. "What are you doing in uniform today?" he asked.

"I had to get a haircut and I stopped in the office to check on a few things," Travis said. "The wedding is hours away and there's not much for the groom to do but show up and say his lines when the time comes."

"I think Lacy is upstairs getting her nails done or something," Brodie said.

"That's okay. I really came by to take another look at the crime scene." Travis scanned the area around the house. "The searchers never found any sign of Alex last night, but I can't shake the feeling that he's hiding somewhere close by."

"We're all keeping an eye out for him," Brodie said.

Travis nodded. "I think I'll go in and check in with Lacy," he said. "She's a little stressed about all of this. I think she's worried I'm going to leave her at the altar or something."

"You wouldn't do that," Brodie said.

"Of course not." Travis moved past him. "Not permanently, anyway."

Brodie headed to his cabin, telling himself Emily might have gone there in search of something she had left behind the night before, maybe. But the place was empty, though the scent of her perfume lingered in the rumpled sheets on the bed, recalling their night together and how much she had come to mean to him.

He turned on his heel and headed to the barn. Maybe she had gone to check on her horse. But Witchy was contentedly munching hay in her stall. The mare swiveled her head to look at Brodie when he leaned over the stall door. She shook her head and whinnied, as if impatient that he was invading her home. "Next time, I'll bring you a carrot," he said, and headed back to the house.

After checking that no one was lurking around to ask him what he was up to, he made his way up the stairs to Emily's bedroom. Five years ago, he had done much the same thing, sneaking past Emily's parents to rendezvous in her room, embracing the role of the dangerous bad boy up to no good with his best friend's sister.

He was cautious this time, not because he thought he had to hide what he was doing, but because he didn't want to upset and alarm the family if there was no need. He knocked softly on the door and relief surged through him as footsteps approached from the other side.

Mrs. Milligan blinked at him, her hair in curlers and some kind of greenish cream on her face. Brodie took a step back. "Have you, um, seen Emily?" he asked.

"No, I haven't."

"Thanks." He backed away, then turned and hurried down the stairs, heart pounding. Something had happened to Emily. She was gone. Now it was time to panic.

"WHERE ARE YOU taking me?"

Alex hadn't bothered to gag Emily, though he had bound her hands and feet with tape, holding her in an iron grip that had left bruises on her upper arms. He had dragged her through the woods to a dirty white van and belted her into the back seat, her head at an uncomfortable angle, every jolt of the vehicle on the uneven ground sending pain through her bound arms.

"You'll see." Alex, his head almost completely covered by a knit cap pulled low and a scarf wound over his mouth, nearly vibrated with suppressed elation. "The sheriff and his deputies were so sure they could stop me this time," he said. "They don't realize who they're dealing with. I'm an expert who's making them look like a bunch of amateurs."

"Why would you want to be an expert at murder?" Emily asked. "You're smart enough you could have excelled at almost anything." She figured it couldn't hurt to flatter him—and as long as they were talking, she could remain alive. Brodie would have missed her by now. He and the others would be looking for her. All she had to do was stay alive until they found her.

"Murder is the ultimate crime," Alex said. "The one that captures everyone's attention and focuses all the effort and money on the killer." He pounded the steering wheel with the heel of his hand. "Talk about a rush."

"Why come to Eagle Mountain?" Emily asked. "Couldn't you have gotten away with a lot more in Denver?"

Alex laughed—a maniacal chuckle that made the hair on the back of her neck stand on end. "You don't get it, do you?" he asked. "You're as clueless as the rest of them. Honestly, I expected better of you."

"Get what?"

"I came to this 'middle of nowhere' excuse for a town because of you!"

You came here to kill me. But she couldn't say the words.

"When we first met, I was intrigued," he said. "You were pretty and smart, and you had a certain *fragile* quality I appreciated. I thought about asking you out, but as I observed you, I noticed that you didn't appear to date anyone—male or female. If I asked you out, chances were you would turn me down. And sex wasn't what I was really after. No, I wanted a much deeper connection. Do you know what that is?"

"No." She had to force the single syllable out. Alex's words terrified her even more than his actions. He had seemed so normal on the outside, yet talking with him now, she understood clearly how unhinged he had become.

"Before I kill someone, I look into her eyes and she realizes her life—her very existence—is in my hands. It is the most profound connection I could ever have with another human being. The feeling I have at that moment, the power and, yes, the love, is incredible. I wanted to experience that with you."

She said nothing, no longer wanting to encourage him.

But he didn't need her encouragement. "I decided I needed to work my way up to you," he said. "I had to experiment and perfect my methods."

"What about Tim?" she asked, hoping to change the subject.

More stomach-turning laughter. "I asked him to come with me because I thought he could be my first victim. But he turned out to be useful."

"He helped you murder the first few women."

"He did. Turns out, he had a taste for killing and I was able to exploit that. Of course, he was nowhere near my level of genius. Which is why he was caught in the end." He giggled. That was the only way Emily could think to describe the sound he made, like a little child chuckling over a silly cartoon. "Things kept getting better and better for me after I came here. The local sheriff's department was as tiny as the town, and they had tiny brains, too. And then I found out your older brother was the sheriff. Such delicious synchronicity. As if this was all meant to be."

He had turned onto the highway up Dixon Pass. Emily craned her head to see out the window. "Is the pass open now?" she asked.

"It doesn't matter if it is," Alex said. "We're not going all the way to the top."

Emily strained forward, staring down the empty road. They passed a sign warning of the road closure, then the orange barricades loomed in sight. But before they reached the barricades, Alex jerked the steering wheel to the right and the van lurched to the side. Unable to brace herself with her bound hands and feet, she jerked painfully forward against the seat belt and her head bounced against the window. Tears stung her eyes from the pain.

The van jolted to a stop, the vehicle's nose buried in a snowbank. Alex shut off the engine, then came around and slid open the side door. He leaned in to unbuckle Emily and she wondered if she could find a way to fight him off. But then he was pulling her from the vehicle. He dumped her into the snow like an old suitcase and slammed the door shut behind her.

"Come on," he said, then grabbed her by the ankles and began dragging her through the snow.

She screamed, hoping to attract the attention of one of the highway workers who were clearing the pass. "Shut up," Alex said, no heat in the words. He climbed over a snowbank and came down in a narrow alley cut through the snow. The passage was just wide enough for one person to walk. He strode down it, dragging Emily by her heels after him. The packed snow scraped her body and sent stabbing pains through her arms. The cold bit into her until her teeth were chattering, and tears streamed down her face from the pain as her head repeatedly pounded against the ground. She wanted to protest, to beg him to stop hurting her, but what difference would it make? He was going to kill her, unless Brodie and Travis and the others got here in time.

Then, as suddenly as he had started, Alex stopped. Emily lay in the snow, staring up at the blue, blue sky, wondering if this would be the last sight she would ever see. Alex came and bent over her, the scarf no longer hiding his face. "Wait for me at the bottom," he said, then gave her a hard shove.

She flew down a steep slope, over the packed snow, sliding on her back, and then she was falling, tumbling. She pressed her arms tightly to her body and tried to curl into a fetal position, sure she was going to break something. Her body turned and bounced and slid some more, until at last she came to rest in a drift of snow, so cold she could no longer shake, numb with fear and the certainty of impending death.

Then Alex was standing beside her. "Was that fun?" he asked. "It looked like it might be." He hauled her upright and tossed her over his shoulder, as if she weighed no more than a sack of flour. "One more trip and we'll be home."

She heard the sound of a motor coming to life, and the creak of turning gears. She craned her head to look and saw an old ski lift with chairs wide enough for two people. Alex shoved Emily into one of the chairs, then sat beside her, and they started up at a rapid clip. She thought of jumping from the lift, but the fall would probably hurt, and with her hands and feet still taped, she wouldn't be able to get away. "Is this where you've been living?" she asked.

"Pretty cool, huh?" he asked. "I got the old ski lift going, and I fixed up the lift shack at the top as a cozy little hideaway."

"Did you set off the avalanche the day Brodie and Gage came here?" she asked.

"They were stupid enough to come here when the avalanche danger was so high. I figure I did a public service, reminding them."

"Are you going to kill me up there?" Emily asked. Maybe it was a stupid question, but she wanted to know. If he answered yes, maybe she would risk jumping off the lift, and find a way to take him with her. With luck, he'd be the one to break a bone or hit his head when they landed.

"I'm going to kill you eventually," he said. "That's the point, isn't it? But not right away. First, we're going to wait."

"Wait for what?"

"For your brother and his men to come after you. I have a big surprise in store for them."

Chapter Seventeen

Brodie descended the stairs two at a time. He met Bette crossing the living room. "Have you seen Gage or Cody?" he asked.

"They and the other groomsmen went into town to pick up their tuxes. And I think they were all going to have lunch together. Why?"

He shook his head and went past her, back onto the porch. He could call Gage and break up the lunch—and probably end up disrupting the whole wedding. Or he could try to locate Emily and Alex on his own, and summon help then. He surveyed the empty porch again, then moved into the yard and parking area. He was staring at the ground, trying to find what might be Emily's footprints, when he spotted something he hadn't noticed before.

He picked up the box of staples, a cold piercing him that had nothing to do with the outside temperature. Something protruded from the corner of the box. He lifted the lid and shuddered as a small white card fluttered to the ground. He could read the words printed on it without bending over: *ICE COLD*.

Alex had Emily, and he wanted Brodie and the others to know he had her. Maybe he even wanted them to come after him.

Brodie picked up the card and tucked it back into the box of staples, then slipped them into his pocket. He surveyed the snow near where the card had fallen, the surface smooth and undisturbed. But a short distance away, he spotted an area of churned-up ice, with drag marks leading away from it.

He followed the marks for several hundred yards, to a wooded area on the edge of the Walker property. Someone had parked a vehicle here, the impressions from the tire tread making a distinctive pattern in the snow, dripping oil forming dark Rorschach blots between the treads. The tracks circled back to the road that led away from the ranch. When Brodie reached the road, he turned and jogged back toward the house to retrieve his truck. Travis's SUV was still parked in front of the house, but the sheriff must still be inside.

Good. Brodie would follow Alex, and once he found him, he'd call for help. And heaven help the man if he hurt one hair on Emily's head.

The oil drip made Alex's tracks relatively easy to follow. Brodie wondered once again if Alex had planned it that way. The man didn't seem to do anything by accident. Had he set up an ambush to take down any law enforcement who followed him? Did he really think he could defeat a whole phalanx of lawmen? Maybe he thought Emily would be enough of a shield to protect him.

The idea made Brodie's stomach churn, but he told himself if Alex intended to use Emily as a shield, he would keep her alive as long as she was useful to him. And no matter what the murderer thought, he wasn't going to be able to outwit and outrun them much longer.

The oil drips turned onto the highway leading up to Dixon Pass. Brodie followed them, keeping his speed down, watching the roadsides for any sign of Alex or Emily, or anything that looked like a trap. Alex might be in disguise, or he might use other people to help him, as he had done before. But Brodie saw no other traffic or pedestrians as the road climbed toward the pass. He sped by the sign warning of the road closure, and was almost to the barricades when he spotted an old van, nose first in the snowbank that marked the site of the avalanche he and Gage had been caught in.

He pulled the truck in behind the van, blocking it, then sat for a long moment, staring at the empty vehicle, noting the puddle of oil beneath the rear axle and the opened passenger-side sliding door. The van had no license plate, and was scratched and battered, the bumper wired in place and a deep scratch running the length of the driver's side. Minutes passed, with no sign of life from the vehicle, and no sound but the ticking of the truck's cooling engine.

Weapon drawn, Brodie eased open the door and

exited the truck, then approached the van. The vehicle was empty, the keys dangling in the ignition. A glance inside showed a roll of duct tape on the back floorboard, and a single long, dark hair caught in a tear in the upholstery on the back seat. Brodie stared at the hair, struggling to rein in his emotions. Emily had been in this van. So where was she now?

The deep snow made it easy to follow a set of footprints and drag marks from the van, up over a berm of snow to a perfectly carved channel, just wide enough for one man to pass through.

Brodie crept down this channel, the cold closing in around him, as if he were passing through a freezer. He kept his weapon drawn, alert for any activity over and above him. But the only sound was the heavy inhale and exhale of his own breath.

He emerged at the top of a rise and stared down at the old Dixon Downhill ski resort. As before, all was silent. A single chair dangled from the old lift and no life stirred below him.

Except... He sniffed the air. Yes, that was smoke, rising in a thin ribbon from a stovepipe on the other side of the canyon, where the old ski lift shack huddled at the top of the lift line. Brodie stared at the smoke, a vise clamped around his heart. Then he turned and walked back to his truck, where, fingers shaking so hard he could hardly make them work, he punched in Gage's number. After three rings, Gage answered. "What's up?" he asked, the sounds of laughter behind him.

"I've found Alex," Brodie said. "He's got Emily. We've got to stop him before it's too late."

ALEX FED MORE wood into the cast-iron stove that crouched at one end of the lift shack, until the flames leaped and popped, the heat almost overpowering, even though Emily was sprawled on the bench seat from an old pickup truck that had been placed in the opposite corner of the little wooden building. Alex—or someone else—had also brought in a rusting metal table, two wooden stools and a cot draped in blankets, presumably where Alex slept. "They should be able to see the smoke from the highway," he said, closing the door of the stove and standing. "I did everything I could to draw them here, but they're so dim, I need to practically lead them by the hand."

"There'll be more of them than there are you," she said. "You can't kill them all."

He turned to face her, firelight reflecting in his eyes, making him look as insane as he probably was. "But I can." He swept a hand toward the slope opposite them. "I've got explosives planted everywhere on that slope. I stole the dynamite and fuses from the highway crew. They use them to set off avalanches when the road is closed. There's enough gunpowder out there to take out half the mountain."

"If you do that, you'll be killed, too," she said.

"I'll be gone before it blows. Of course, you'll still be here." He tilted his head, studying her. "Do you think I should kill you before I go—or let you die with your brothers in the explosions?"

She closed her eyes, unwilling to look at his face any longer. The mania in his eyes frightened her. Had the insanity been there all along and she had simply failed to see it, believing he was just another undergrad, not someone she really noticed?

"They're here." She opened her eyes at his words, in time to see him pick up a rifle and carry it to the sliding window that filled half of one side of the shack. Originally, the window had allowed the lift operator a view of the lift line and the skiers unloading at the top of the lift. Now it gave Alex a view back toward the opposite slope, beyond which the van was parked. "They're really going to make this too easy for me," he said, sliding the window open a few inches.

She tried to rise up and look past him out the window, but the pain in her arms and legs made movement difficult. The best she could manage was a view of the sky and the back of his head.

Without warning, a blast echoed through the shack. Emily screamed. Alex steadied the rifle against his shoulder and fired again. The smell of gunpowder filled the air, and cold from the open window settled over her like an icy blanket. Alex straightened and laughed. "You should see them out there, running around like frightened rabbits," he said. "I can't believe they thought they were just going to walk up here and take me."

door to the stove and tossed the phone inside. The smell of burning plastic filled the air.

"Isn't that noble of him, wanting to take your place?" Alex said.

Emily didn't have words to explain how Brodie's offer made her feel. Was he only doing his job as an officer of the law, or did she really mean that much to him?

BRODIE, GAGE, DWIGHT, Jamie, Nate, Ryder and Marshal Cody Rankin gathered at the top of the rise looking down onto the ski lift, just out of range of Alex's rifle. Brodie punched Emily's number again and listened to it ring and ring. "He probably really did destroy the phone," Ryder, who was standing next to Brodie, said. "He doesn't strike me as one to bluff."

"Maybe we should get Travis out here to talk to him," Dwight said.

"Not yet," Gage said. "Rob is with him. His job is to keep him occupied and in the dark." DEA agent Rob Allerton was Paige Riddell's boyfriend and had the least involvement of any of them in this case.

"Alex might make a deal with Travis," Dwight said.

"He's more likely to kill him," Gage said. "I promised Lacy I'd do my best to see that she wasn't a widow before she was a wife."

"How are we going to get closer to him?" Nate asked.

"The snow down in the valley must be six feet

deep," Jamie said. "You'd never get through there without a snow machine. Even if you could somehow manage on snowshoes, you'd have to climb down there first, and Alex would have plenty of time to see you and pick you off."

"How did he get up to the lift shack?" Brodie asked, studying the steep, rocky incline from the bottom of the lift to the top. "And how did he get Emily up there with him?"

"I think they rode the lift," Dwight said.

"The lift's broken," Gage said. "It hasn't worked in years."

"Maybe he figured out how to get it running," Brodie said. "Didn't you say it's powered by an old car motor?"

"That doesn't help us," Nate said. "If we try to start the lift, he'll just shoot us. He can let us get almost to him and pick us off."

"Maybe we could lure him out of the shack and pick him off with sniper fire," Ryder said.

"He'd never come out of that lift shack," Gage said. "Not without Emily as a shield. He's too smart for that."

"I still say we need to get Travis here to talk to him," Dwight said.

Brodie studied the scene below him while those around him debated the best approach. "What if instead of climbing up to him, we climb down?" he asked after a moment.

"Climb down from where?" Jamie asked.

"From above the lift shack." He indicated the cliff that rose behind the shack, part of a long ridge that formed the east side of the pass. "That may be how Alex got down there in the first place. He's a rock climber, right?"

"How would you even get there?" Gage asked, squinting at the mountain that rose above the lift shack.

"There's an old mining road that runs along there, just above the ski area," Nate said. "See that narrow ledge." He pointed, and Brodie thought he could make out the relatively horizontal path along the cliff face. "Climbers use it in the summer. You can take a Jeep up there then, but you'd have to snowshoe in now."

"And if Alex did turn around and see someone up there, he could pick them off with that rifle." Gage shook his head. "It's too risky."

"He hasn't got a view of the slope behind him from the lift shack," Brodie said. "He'd have to step outside to see anyone up there, and we've already established he's unlikely to do that. The thing we need to do is keep him distracted."

"How?" Jamie asked.

"We could take turns approaching behind cover and taking potshots at him," Dwight said. "Or launch flares at him."

"Have to be careful with that," Nate said. "You don't want to set off another avalanche."

"Okay, so we could probably distract him,"

Dwight said. "But who are we going to get to make the climb? It looks pretty technical."

"I've done some climbing," Brodie said. All of it in a gym, but they didn't have to know that. He knew how to use the equipment, and he was desperate to get Emily out of there before she suffered even more than she already had.

"It's too risky." Gage shook his head.

"It's our best chance of getting to him," Brodie said. "He won't be expecting it because he sees himself as the expert and we're all the amateurs. He's probably made the climb, but he believes we'd never attempt it."

"He's right. You shouldn't attempt it," Dwight said.

"If it was Brenda trapped there, would you do it?" Brodie asked.

Dwight compressed his lips together. "I don't know," he said after a moment. "I'm just glad my wife isn't in there with him."

Emily wasn't Brodie's wife, but if things had worked out differently, she might have been. He wasn't going to let her die if he could do something—even a crazy, reckless stunt like rappelling down an icy cliff—to save her.

He turned to Gage. "Where can I get climbing gear?"

Nate clapped Brodie on the shoulder. "I've got a friend who can fix you up."

"Then let's go. We don't have any time to waste."

Chapter Eighteen

Alex paced back and forth across the floor of the lift shack, alternately cursing to himself and stopping to stare out the window. "Why aren't they doing anything?" he asked. "Nobody up there has moved for the past half an hour." He turned back to Emily. "Maybe they've decided to just let you die. What do you think about that?"

She swallowed and held her head up, though every movement sent pain shooting through her. Alex had let the fire go out and the cold made the pain worse. She couldn't stop shivering, but Alex, dressed in a fleece top and jeans, didn't seem to notice. "Maybe they went to get Travis," she said. "You burned my phone, so they don't have any way of letting you know."

"They better not be planning any tricks. They'll find out soon enough they can't trick me. Do you know why I chose this place for this standoff?" He put his face very close to hers, so that she could smell his stale body odor. It must have been a while since he had showered. How long had he been living up here in this primitive shack? "Do you know?" he demanded.

"No."

"It's because that road up there—" he gestured with the rifle he still held "—that road is the only way in here." He laughed. "Unless they decided to try to land a helicopter down here. Not easy, and if they do, I'll just set off the explosives as soon as it touches down." He returned to watching out the window. "They can't get at me any other way."

"If they can't get in, how are you going to get out?" she asked.

He grinned, the expression in his eyes telling her he was long past any concrete grip on reality. "I'm going to climb out." He gestured behind them. "That cliff is a 5.9, maybe a 5.10 route. Expert only. But I've done it half a dozen times. I could do it with my eyes closed. By the time I make it to the top, they'll be trapped down here under tons of rock. I'll be far away from here, with a new identity, before anyone even starts to look for me."

"It sounds like you've thought of everything." She was back to flattery—anything to keep him talking and get on his good side.

"Of course I have. It's how I've been so successful so far. These country rubes aren't used to dealing with genius."

"You told them on the phone that you had a game for them to play," she said.

"For the sheriff. Of course, it's a game he can't win. I'm not stupid enough to design it any other way."

She wet her dry, cracking lips. "What is the game?"

"He has to guess the way I've planned for him to die."

"Why would he want to play a game like that?"

"If he guesses right, I'll slit your throat and you'll die quickly. If he guesses wrong…" He let the words trail away, leaving her to imagine the dozens of ways he might choose to make her suffer. She pushed the thoughts away. She wasn't dead yet. She wasn't going to give up hope. A person could live a long time on hope, or so she had read.

Hurry, she sent the thought to whatever rescuers might be mustering to help her. *Hurry, because I don't know how much longer I can hang on.*

"I've done this climb before, but not with the snow and ice." Nate's friend, a wiry thirtysomething who went by the single name Truman, handed Brodie a climbing helmet. "You're certifiable if you want to do it now."

"I don't have any choice." Brodie tugged the helmet on and fastened the chin strap, then reached for a pair of climbing gloves.

"We could try to bring in a helicopter," Nate said. "I bet he'd come outside when he heard that. We could probably get a good shot at him from inside the chopper."

"Or he could decide to kill Emily then and there." Brodie pulled a down jacket over his wool sweater. A Kevlar vest and thermal underwear added extra protection from the cold and gunfire, though he had doubts the vest would stop a bullet from a high-powered rifle—or prevent him from breaking every bone in his body if he fell from the cliff.

"The safety harness should protect you from a fall." Truman demonstrated hooking into the safety line. "It won't help if you bash into the rocks while you're swinging there, but if you lose contact with the cliff, we'll do our best to haul you up."

"I feel so much better now," Brodie said.

Truman made a face and ran through a checklist of the gear. None of the terms were new to Brodie, and he was beginning to feel more confident. "Come on," he said. "We need to get to the site where I'll start the downclimb." Every minute that passed was another minute that might cause Alex to lose patience and take his frustration out on Emily.

They drove as far as they could in Truman's Jeep, then strapped on snowshoes for the rest of the journey. They had to snowshoe almost two miles until they reached a point directly above the lift shack. Brodie peered down at the little tin-roofed building. "There's no smoke coming out of the stovepipe now," he said.

Nate was on the phone with Gage and relayed Brodie's observation. "Gage says Alex and Emily are still in there. He can see them through his binoculars."

"What are they doing?" Brodie asked.

"Just sitting there, he says. Waiting."

"Somebody's been climbing this route recently." Truman pulled back a tarp underneath a spindly fir to reveal a pair of snowshoes.

"Alex," Brodie said. "I figured he had to be getting to and from the shack this way, at least part of the time."

"Then you might be in luck," Truman said. "He may have set anchors in the rock that you can hook on to. Watch for areas cleared of snow—that might mark his hand- and footholds."

Brodie nodded and focused on checking and double-checking his safety harness.

"Why can't he just rappel down?" Nate asked. "It seems like that would be a lot faster."

"It would, if the cliff was straight down," Truman said. "But it's not. There are a lot of rocks and trees and stuff that stick out. Try to rappel that and you'll just smash into stuff. No, our man is going to have to downclimb." He grinned at Brodie. "Sucks to be you, dude."

Brodie grunted and moved to the edge of the cliff. "You two just hang on if I slip."

Truman moved up beside him. "The route is hard to see from this angle," he said. "We're sort of jutting out over most of the area you'll be descending. But there's a ledge about fifteen feet down that will be a good place to stop and rest."

"If we can't see him, how are we going to know what to do to help him?" Nate asked.

"You can get a good idea of what's happening by the feel of the ropes." Truman clapped Brodie on the back. "Ready?"

Brodie nodded. His brain was telling him he was crazy to risk his life this way, but he was ignoring his brain. His heart was saying he didn't have a choice, and he was choosing to go with his heart. "Tell the others it's time to start whatever they've come up with to distract Alex."

"I've told them," Nate said. "Good luck."

The first step off the cliff, blindly groping for a foothold in the slick rock, was the worst. Relief surged through him as his foot found purchase and he was able to steady himself, but he couldn't stop to enjoy the sensation. He had to keep going. Glancing down, he could see the shallow rock ledge Truman had mentioned, and he focused on getting to it. One foot here, one hand there. Test the next foothold to see if it would support his weight. Reject another foothold as too weak or too slick. He wedged his foot into a niche in the rock. It felt secure, so he lowered himself down, searching for the next foothold.

Then the rock gave way. He flailed around, seeking purchase and finding none, swinging free against the rock face, like a pendulum in a crazy clock. Truman, very pale and very far away, looked over from the top. They had agreed that they couldn't shout to one another for fear of attracting Alex's attention.

Nate also leaned out and gave him a thumbs-up. Truman pointed to the ledge and pantomimed lowering the rope. Brodie nodded. They were going to lower him to the ledge. Good idea.

Once safely on the ledge, he rested a moment, his body plastered to the rock, the cold seeping into him despite the layers of clothing. In contrast, the sun at his back burned. When he was breathing more or less regularly again, he tugged on the rope, a signal that he was ready to start down once more.

He fell three more times on the way down, each time the safety harness catching him, the rope stretching and bouncing him slightly. He learned to relax until the swaying slowed, then to find purchase in the rock once more. As Truman had guessed, Alex had hammered pitons into the rock face, allowing Brodie to clip into these as he moved down the cliff, untethering from Truman and Nate above.

About three-quarters of the way down he realized he was no longer afraid. He was actually doing this. The adrenaline rush was exhilarating, and if what awaited him at the end of the climb wasn't so important, he might have lingered to enjoy himself.

But he had no time to indulge himself. He moved as quickly as possible. When he touched ground only a dozen feet behind the lift shack, his hand shook as he unhooked from the safety rope and climbed out of the harness. He took the time to roll up everything and stash it underneath a tree, not wanting to provide an escape route if Alex managed to make it out of the lift shack before Brodie got to him.

He straightened, drew his weapon and started toward the shack. His plan was to go in, surprise Alex and make an arrest with no one getting hurt. It was a good plan, but he had no idea if it would really work.

EMILY HAD FALLEN into a kind of stupor on the old car seat, while Alex slumped on a stool in front of the window, the rifle propped against the wall beside him. Earlier, she had spent some time groping around the seat, hoping to find a popped spring or a protruding bit of metal to cut the tape at her wrists or ankles, but no such luck. All she could do was wait and pray. She tried asking Alex questions about himself, but after a while he had stopped answering her.

Suddenly, he shoved back the stool and stood. "It's about time," he said.

Emily pushed herself up straighter. "What's happening?" she asked.

Alex gestured toward the window. "They've found a way to communicate."

By arching her back and craning her neck, Emily was able to make out someone holding what looked like a poster with writing on it. But it was too far away to read. "What does it say?" she asked.

Alex pulled out a pair of binoculars and studied the sign. "*THE SHERIFF IS READY TO TALK*."

"Travis is there?" Emily's heart pounded. Travis shouldn't be here! He should be with Lacy, getting married.

Alex scowled. "There's someone there in a sheriff's department uniform, with a big hat and a star on his chest, but I can't tell if it's your brother." He set down the binoculars and looked around the lift shack. "I need something to write on. I need to tell him to move in closer—and to take off the stupid hat."

"You should have thought of that before you burned up my phone." Emily braced herself for another blow, but Alex only scowled at her and began digging through the debris against the walls of the shack. Amazingly, he came up with a small whiteboard, roughly two-foot square. Emily recalled seeing similar boards at lift shacks at other resorts, used to convey messages such as "Mr. Reynolds, contact child care" or "New snow overnight 4 inches!"

In a drawer, Alex found a set of dry-erase markers. He scrawled his message, *COME CLOSER AND TAKE OFF THE HAT.*

"They're not going to be able to see that from in here," Emily said. "You'll have to go outside."

"And give them a clear shot at me?" Alex shook his head. "No, you'll go out." He pulled the knife from his belt and she shrank back in fear. But he bent and cut the tape from her ankles, then did the same for her wrists.

She cried out as she brought her hands in front of her again, the stabbing pain doubling her over.

Alex chafed her ankles between his hands. "You'll be fine in a minute." He straightened and thrust the sign and the marker at her. "Go out there and hold this up. And don't try anything. If you run, I'll shoot you in the back." He held up the rifle.

She gripped the board with numb, aching fingers and he tucked the marker into the pocket of her jeans and hauled her to her feet. She could barely walk, much less run. Alex took her arm and dragged her toward the door of the lift shack. "Get out there!" he called, and thrust her out the door.

She landed sprawling in the snow, the sign face-down beside her. "Get up!" Alex shouted, and she looked back to see the rifle pointed at her.

Clenching her teeth, she shoved to her knees, then slowly stood, bringing the sign with her. Holding on to the lift shack for support, she made her way around to the side facing the road, moving through snow that came past her knees. Finally she stopped and held up the sign. Seconds later, an answer appeared: *YOU OKAY?* in letters large enough to be seen clearly even at that distance.

She nodded, hoping someone was watching through binoculars. Then she scrawled *YES* beneath Alex's message. A cold wind buffeted her, and she was shaking so badly she had trouble holding on to the sign. "Get back in here!" Alex shouted.

She wanted to ignore the command, to run as fast and as far as she could. But that wouldn't be very far. The snow here was several feet deep and she could scarcely move. She would be dead before she took more than a few steps.

"Get in!" Alex shouted again.

Instead, she moved up against the lift shack once more, the thick logs providing a barrier to the wind and, she hoped, bullets from the man inside. She sank into the snow and sat, arms wrapped around her knees. Alex couldn't see her from here, and he wouldn't be able to shoot her without coming outside—something he apparently was loath to do. She would sit here until her strength returned and some of the pain in her limbs subsided. By then, maybe someone below would have come up here to her, or found a way to get to her. Having her out of the way might even help them.

Alex was screaming now, a stream of profanities aimed at her. She closed her eyes and shut him out, focusing instead on the whistle of the wind around the corner of the lift shack, and the creak of the chair on the overhead cable.

And the sound of footsteps moving through the snow.

Her eyes snapped open, fear choking her. Alex's rage at her must have overcome his fear of leaving the shack. But instead of Alex, she was amazed to see Brodie standing at the corner of the shack, one finger to his lips. "How?" She had scarcely uttered the single syllable before he shook his head. He motioned for her to stay where she was, and indicated he intended to go inside the shack.

She shook her head. If Brodie went in there, Alex

would kill him. He had the rifle, and a knife, and then there were the explosives everywhere on the mountain. How could she warn Brodie without Alex overhearing? She picked up the sign and rubbed out the message there with the sleeve of her sweater, then wrote, *HE HAS EXPLOSIVES ALL OVER THE MOUNTAIN. WILL DETONATE.*

Brodie read the message and nodded. Then his eyes met hers, and the determination and, yes, love in that single glance made her almost giddy. Then he was gone, around the back of the shack once more.

Emily shoved to her feet. She couldn't sit here, not knowing what was happening with Brodie and Alex. She followed Brodie around the back of the shack, floundering through the thick snow, which covered the sound of her approach. At the door of the shack he stopped, weapon raised, then burst inside.

She braced herself for the blast of gunfire or the sounds of a struggle, but only ringing silence followed. Cautiously, she moved forward, until she was just outside the open door. "What's happening?" she called.

"He isn't here," Brodie called. He stood over the table, examining the items scattered across it. "He must have slipped out while I was with you."

"A very good deduction," Alex said as he grabbed Emily from behind and put a knife to her throat.

This can't be happening, Emily thought, as Alex crushed her against him. The knife bit into her throat, but she scarcely felt it, as if her body was becoming immune to pain.

"Let her go," Brodie said, his gun leveled at Alex.

"Drop the gun or she dies now." Alex pulled her more tightly against him, so that she could hardly breathe, her body angled so that she was between his legs, one hand almost resting on his groin.

Brodie tossed the gun aside. It sank out of sight in the snow. "What now?" he asked.

"That's right," Alex said. "I'm calling the shots."

Emily gripped the dry-erase marker in her hand. As weapons went, it was pathetic. But it was all she had. Several years before, when she was an undergrad, she had attended a presentation on self-defense. All she could remember was the instructor's advice to use whatever was at hand as a weapon. Most of the feeling had returned to her fingers. She made a fist around the marker, then drove it as hard as she could into Alex's groin.

The knife slid across her throat, but she was able to shove out of Alex's grasp as he doubled over. Brodie jumped on him and the two grappled in the snow. Emily knelt by the shack, watching in horror as blood stippled the pristine surface of the snow with red.

The two men rolled over and over in the snow, first Brodie on top, then Alex. With a cry of rage, Alex heaved Brodie off him and jumped to his feet. Then he was running, headed for the cliff. He began to climb, clambering up the steep slope without aid of harness or ropes or even gloves.

Brodie knelt beside Emily. "It's bleeding a lot, but I don't think the cuts are too deep," he said. He stripped out of his jacket, peeled off his sweater and wrapped it around her neck.

"There's a rifle in the shack," she said through chattering teeth. "You need to get it and go after him."

"It's okay," he said, one arm wrapped around her. "Nate and another man are waiting at the top of the cliff. He won't get away from them."

They stared as Alex scaled the cliff, swarming up the rock face. Emily gasped as he slipped, then regained his foothold. "He's going too fast," Brodie said. "He's being reckless."

He was almost to the top, where the rock jutted out and he had to pull himself over it. He had almost made it when something at the top caught his attention. "It's Nate," Brodie said. "He's got him covered."

A rope dropped over the edge of the cliff and dangled beside Alex. "Nate will pull him up and arrest him," Brodie said.

But Alex didn't take the rope. Instead, he looked back over his shoulder. He took one hand from the rock and balanced for a second, before releasing the other hand and falling backward.

Emily buried her face in Brodie's shoulder. Alex's cries echoed around them, then all fell silent. "Is he dead?" she asked.

"If he isn't, he's badly hurt." He stood. "Gage is

sending a couple of snowmobiles down to get us. Let's go meet them."

"Can we sit here a little bit, until they get here?" she asked.

"Are you too weak to walk?" His voice rose in alarm. "Do you want me to carry you?"

"No, I don't want you to carry me." The idea made her want to laugh.

"What's so funny?."

"I'm wondering if there's a statute of limitations on proposals."

He hesitated, then said. "What do you mean?"

She pressed her palms to his chest, over his heart, and looked into his eyes. "I mean, I don't want you to carry me. But I might want you to marry me."

"Because I scaled a cliff and faced death to save you?"

"Because you did those things. And because I love you. More than I was willing to admit before."

"Why weren't you willing to admit it?"

"Are you always so full of questions?"

"I want to be sure you're not out of your mind from loss of blood."

"I turned down your proposal before because I was afraid of what I would have to give up if we married," she said. "Now I'm old enough to see that marriage isn't about giving things up—it's about gaining a partner who can help you get even more out of life."

He gently brushed her hair back from her face

and looked into her eyes. "Emily Walker, will you marry me?" he asked.

Tears—of relief, and such joy she could hardly contain it—flooded her eyes and she pressed her lips to his.

The roar of an approaching snowmobile interrupted their kiss. Two more snowmobiles followed. They stopped nearby and Gage pulled off his helmet. "Are you okay?" he asked.

"Emily's wounded," Brodie said. "I'm fine." He looked toward the cliff. "Alex is either dead or wounded."

The man on the second snowmobile collected a medical kit from the back of the machine and started through the snow toward the cliff. The driver of the third snowmobile, a woman, approached Emily. "Let's take a look," she said, and began to unwind Brodie's sweater. She surveyed the wound. "It's mostly stopped bleeding. You might need a few stitches and you might be more comfortable wearing scarves for a while, but in a year or two I'll bet the scar hardly shows."

"I'll take a scar over the alternative," she said.

"I'll just get you cleaned up a bit," the woman said, and opened her medical kit.

The other paramedic returned, shaking his head. "That one doesn't need me anymore," he said.

Emily tried to feel some sympathy or sorrow for the man Alex might have been—handsome, smart, with every advantage. But she felt only emptiness.

She didn't have it in her to hate someone so twisted, but she could admit she was relieved he would never terrorize anyone else again.

The paramedic helped her to the snowmobile and assisted her in climbing on. Brodie rode behind Gage. They were at the top again before Emily remembered one of the most important questions of the day. She looked at Gage. "Where is Travis?"

Gage checked his watch. "I hope he's getting married about now."

"But you're the best man," she said. "And I'm one of the bridesmaids."

"I think they can finish the ceremony without us," Gage said.

"He's going to be furious when he finds out what happened," Emily said.

"He is. But he'll get over it."

"Get over what?"

They turned to see Travis, a leather duster pulled on over his tux, striding toward them. Lacy, a down parka over her wedding dress, and the rest of the wedding party trailed behind. "What are you doing here?" Gage demanded.

"I came to see this case to the finish." He turned to Emily. "Are you okay?"

She nodded. "I'll be fine." At least, she would be, given time to rest and heal.

Travis nodded and turned back to Gage. "Alex?"

"He's dead."

"He jumped off the cliff, rather than face arrest," Brodie said.

"It's over," Emily said, the impact just beginning to hit her. "It's really over."

"It is." Gage put one arm around his brother. "You can leave the mop-up to us. Now you can get on with the honeymoon."

"We have to get married first," Lacy said.

"You're not married yet?" Emily asked.

"We couldn't get married with most of the wedding party—and some of the guests—up here on the pass," she said.

"You all weren't coming to the wedding, so we decided to bring the wedding to you," Bette said. She indicated everyone around them. "We're all here, but it's a little chilly, so let's get going, why don't we?"

Emily put a hand to her throat. "But I'm not dressed for a wedding."

"No one is looking at you." Bette handed her a bouquet. "Now hold this, stand over there. Lacy, you stand here."

Bette arranged everyone, and within five minutes Emily was blinking back tears as her eldest brother and her dear friend promised to love, honor and cherish each other for the rest of their lives. The officiant pronounced them husband and wife and they kissed as a tinny rendition of the Wedding March—courtesy of someone's phone—serenaded them.

"Now everyone come back to the reception," Bette said. Gage started to object, but she held up a hand. "I know what you're going to say. You have a crime scene to process. I'll send refreshments back to you."

"If it's all right with you, I'll stay with Emily," Brodie said.

"You do that," Travis said. "I think I can trust you to take good care of her this time."

"This time, and for every time to come," he said.

The others piled into their vehicles and drove away, Travis and Lacy in a white pickup truck with tin cans tied to the back and *Just Married* scrawled across the back window. Then Brodie walked Emily to the ambulance and climbed in after her. "I don't think you ever gave me an answer to my proposal," he said, taking her hand.

"Yes," she said. "Yes, I'll marry you."

He held her gaze, steady and sure. "I never want to hold you back from your dreams," he said. "I only want to be part of them."

"You are." She kissed him, a sweet meeting of their lips full of promise and hope and all things she was determined to never give up again.

* * * * *

#1893 SAFETY BREACH
Longview Ridge Ranch • by Delores Fossen

Former profiler Gemma Hanson is in witness protection, but she's still haunted by memories of the serial killer who tried to kill her last year. Her concerns skyrocket when Sheriff Kellan Slater tells her the murderer has learned her location and is coming to finish what he started.

#1894 UNDERCOVER ACCOMPLICE
Red, White and Built: Delta Force Deliverance
by Carol Ericson

When Delta Force soldier Hunter Mancini learns the group that kidnapped CIA operative Sue Chandler is now framing his team leader, he asks for her help. But could she be hiding something that would clear his boss?

#1895 AMBUSHED AT CHRISTMAS
Rushing Creek Crime Spree • by Barb Han

After a jogger resembling Detective Leah Cordon is murdered, rancher Deacon Kent approaches her, believing the attack is related to recent cattle mutilations. Can they find the killer before he corners Leah?

#1896 DANGEROUS CONDITIONS
Protectors at Heart • by Jenna Kernan

Former soldier Logan Lynch's first investigation as the constable of a small town leads him to microbiologist Paige Morris, whose boss was killed. Yet as they search for the murderer, Paige is forced to reveal a secret that shows the stakes couldn't be higher.

#1897 RULES IN DEFIANCE
Blackhawk Security • by Nichole Severn

Blackhawk Security investigator Elliot Dunham never expected his neighbor to show up bruised and covered in blood in the middle of the night. To protect Waylynn Hargraves, Elliot must defy the rules he's set for himself, because he knows he's all that stands between her and certain death.

#1898 HIDDEN TRUTH
Stealth • by Danica Winters

When undercover CIA agent Trevor Martin meets Sabrina Parker, the housekeeper at the ranch where he's lying low, he doesn't know she's an undercover FBI agent. After a murder on the property, the operatives must work together, but can they discover their hidden connection before it's too late? _____

Get 4 FREE REWARDS!

We'll send you 2 FREE Books plus 2 FREE Mystery Gifts.

Harlequin Intrigue® books feature heroes and heroines that confront and survive danger while finding themselves irresistibly drawn to one another.

FREE Value Over **$20**

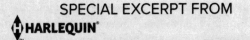
"Why did you say you owed me?" she asked.

The question came out of the blue and threw him, so
much so that he gulped down too much coffee and nearly
choked. Hardly the reaction for a tough-nosed cop. But
his reaction to her hadn't exactly been all badge, either.

Kellan lifted his shoulder and wanted to kick himself
for ever bringing it up in the first place. Bad timing, he
thought, and wondered if there would ever be a good time
for him to grovel.

"I didn't stop Eric from shooting you that night." He
said that fast. Not a drop of sugarcoating. "You, my father
and Dusty. I'm sorry for that."

Her silence and the shimmering look in her eyes made
him stupid, and that was the only excuse he could come
up with for why he kept talking.

"It's easier for me to toss some of the blame at you for not ID'ing a killer sooner," he added. And he still did blame her, in part, for that. "But it was my job to stop him before he killed two people and injured another while he was right under my nose."

The silence just kept on going. So much so that Kellan turned, ready to go back to his desk so that he wouldn't continue to prattle on. Gemma stopped him by putting her hand on his arm. It was like a trigger that sent his gaze searching for hers. Wasn't hard to find when she stood and met him eye to eye.

"It was easier for me to toss some of the blame at you, too." She made another of those sighs. "But there was no stopping Eric that night. The stopping should have happened prior to that. I should have seen the signs." When he started to speak, Gemma lifted her hand to silence him. "And please don't tell me that it's all right, that I'm not at fault. I don't think I could take that right now."

Unfortunately, Kellan understood just what she meant. They were both still hurting, and a mutual sympathyfest was only going to make it harder. They couldn't go back. Couldn't undo. And that left them with only one direction. Looking ahead and putting this son of a bitch in a hole where he belonged.

Don't miss Safety Breach *by Delores Fossen,*
available December 2019 wherever
Harlequin® Intrigue books and ebooks are sold.

Harlequin.com

HSEEXP50496

Need an adrenaline rush from nail-biting tales
(and irresistible males)?

Check out **Harlequin Intrigue®**,
Harlequin® Romantic Suspense and
Love Inspired® Suspense books!

New books available every month!

CONNECT WITH US AT:

Facebook.com/groups/HarlequinConnection

 Facebook.com/HarlequinBooks

 Twitter.com/HarlequinBooks

 Instagram.com/HarlequinBooks

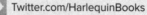 Pinterest.com/HarlequinBooks

ReaderService.com

**ROMANCE WHEN
YOU NEED IT**

SGENRE2018R

Love Harlequin romance?

DISCOVER.

Be the first to find out about promotions, news and exclusive content!

f Facebook.com/HarlequinBooks

Twitter.com/HarlequinBooks

Instagram.com/HarlequinBooks

Pinterest.com/HarlequinBooks

ReaderService.com

EXPLORE.

Sign up for the Harlequin e-newsletter and download a free book from any series at **TryHarlequin.com.**

CONNECT.

Join our Harlequin community to share your thoughts and connect with other romance readers!

Facebook.com/groups/HarlequinConnection

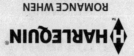

HARLEQUIN™

ROMANCE WHEN
YOU NEED IT

Looking for more satisfying love stories with community and family at their core?

Check out **Harlequin® Special Edition** and **Love Inspired®** books!

New books available every month!

CONNECT WITH US AT:

Facebook.com/groups/HarlequinConnection

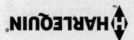

HARLEQUIN®

ROMANCE WHEN
YOU NEED IT

HFGENRE2018